Death of a Mill Girl

"A vivid picture of life in [the] 1830s . . . I for one would enjoy reading the future adventures of Josiah Beede."
—*Reviewing the Evidence*

"Richly realized setting and period details, impeccable plotting, and a wise hero made more appealing by his foibles . . . *Death of a Mill Girl* kept me reading straight through and left me eager for Linsley's next."
—Ann McMillan,
author of *Dead March*

"Captures the atmosphere of a small, early nineteenth century New England town . . . a pleasant evening's reading."
—*I Love a Mystery*

"The book's strength is . . . in the depiction of farm and mill life in mid-nineteenth century New England . . . vividly described."
—*The Mystery Reader*

Berkley Prime Crime titles by Clyde Linsley

DEATH OF A MILL GIRL
SAVING LOUISA
DIE LIKE A HERO

DIE LIKE A HERO

Clyde Linsley

BERKLEY PRIME CRIME, NEW YORK

THE BERKLEY PUBLISHING GROUP
Published by the Penguin Group
Penguin Group (USA) Inc.
375 Hudson Street, New York, New York 10014, USA
Penguin Group (Canada), 10 Alcorn Avenue, Toronto, Ontario M4V 3B2, Canada
(a division of Pearson Penguin Canada Inc.)
Penguin Books Ltd., 80 Strand, London WC2R 0RL, England
Penguin Group Ireland, 25 St. Stephen's Green, Dublin 2, Ireland (a division of Penguin Books Ltd.)
Penguin Group (Australia), 250 Camberwell Road, Camberwell, Victoria 3124, Australia
(a division of Pearson Australia Group Pty. Ltd.)
Penguin Books India Pvt. Ltd., 11 Community Centre, Panchsheel Park, New Delhi—110 017, India
Penguin Group (NZ), Cnr. Airborne and Rosedale Roads, Albany, Auckland 1310, New Zealand
(a division of Pearson New Zealand Ltd.)
Penguin Books (South Africa) (Pty.) Ltd., 24 Sturdee Avenue, Rosebank, Johannesburg 2196, South Africa

Penguin Books Ltd., Registered Offices: 80 Strand, London WC2R 0RL, England

This is a work of fiction. Names, characters, places, and incidents either are the product of the author's imagination or are used fictitiously, and any resemblance to actual persons, living or dead, business establishments, events, or locales is entirely coincidental.

DIE LIKE A HERO

A Berkley Prime Crime Book / published by arrangement with the author

PRINTING HISTORY
Berkley Prime Crime mass-market edition / April 2005

ISBN: 0-425-20003-5

Berkley Prime Crime Books are published by The Berkley Publishing Group,
a division of Penguin Group (USA) Inc.,
375 Hudson Street, New York, New York 10014.
The name BERKLEY PRIME CRIME and the BERKLEY PRIME CRIME design
are trademarks belonging to Penguin Group (USA) Inc.

PRINTED IN THE UNITED STATES OF AMERICA

10 9 8 7 6 5 4 3 2 1

In memoriam, Stan Natanson

"When it comes your time to die, be not like those whose hearts are filled with the fear of death, so that when their time comes they weep and pray for a little more time to live their lives over again in a different way. Sing your death song and die like a hero going home."

Chief Tecumseh, Shawnee Nation,
quoted in Lee Sulzman, *Shawnee History*

Chapter 1

"I take it that he went quickly," said Josiah Beede.

"That is correct," the black-browed man said. He spoke quietly, to avoid disturbing the somber crowd that surrounded them.

"He lasted about a week and a half," Daniel Webster went on. "He called for a doctor on Friday and was dead on a Sunday."

Beede nodded. "His wife is . . ."

"Still in Ohio," said Webster. "She is in poor health, and it was thought best that she wait until later in the spring before making the journey to Washington."

Webster sighed. "Now she needn't come at all. We shall, instead, deliver her husband to her."

They stood in the East Room of the President's House, against the wall and out of the way. Beede sensed that Webster did not care for "out of the way," and would always prefer to be the center of attention, but the mass of people crowding the room made that difficult. William Henry Harrison, Indian fighter, military governor of the Indiana Territory, and now the late President of the United States, lay, in a coffin lined and covered in black and ringed with flowers, on a table in the center of the room. Surrounding the coffin stood members of his cabinet, and ringed behind them were members of the House and Senate and a military honor guard. The room was packed to overflowing. Outside, the city was basking in the first blush of spring. Inside, the heat and the smell of the crowd reminded Beede of the middle of July.

Webster, Beede knew, was eager to join his colleagues in the position of prominence at the center of the room. Indeed, as secretary of state, his position would be preeminent.

"The funeral ceremony is about to begin," Webster said, finally. "I must take my place. Will you remain for a few days? Perhaps you would care to join the funeral procession."

Beede nodded. "I shall follow. I never knew the man, but I feel a certain obligation to anyone who held the position of President, however briefly."

"That's admirable," Webster said. "In fact, I would appreciate it if you could join me this evening for dinner, if you've no pressing engagement elsewhere. There is a matter of some importance I'd like to discuss with you."

Beede was startled. Webster was a Whig, and he certainly would know of Beede's connections to Andrew Jackson and Martin Van Buren. He could not imagine what discussion might ensue between two political opponents.

"I have no pressing engagements," he said. "I came to Washington on personal business and have made no social plans."

"Excellent," said Webster. "My house is directly opposite the President's Park. Come about eight, if you please." He began moving away, clearly eager to take his place among the public mourners.

"May I ask what important matter I should expect to consider?" he asked.

"I'd rather not discuss it in this public place," Webster said over his shoulder. "Let us say simply that it is, in a sense, a matter of life and death—and perhaps the future of the union."

He strode away quickly, leaving Beede to wonder whether the theatricality was necessary.

Chapter 2

The coffin bearing the president's body had been
carried outside to the funeral wagon—not a
hearse, precisely, since none had been available on
short notice—where it was mounted on a pedestal in
full view of the spectators. The wagon was curtained
in black and drawn by six horses, also draped in
black. It was a somber, ceremonial procession. The
death of a president in office had never occurred before, and those who planned the funeral were well
aware that they would be setting a precedent for the
future.

The procession moved slowly away, accompanied
by the pallbearers, government dignitaries, the mildly
curious, and the Marine Band. Beede made ready to
follow them but was stopped by a familiar voice.

"I had heard that you were in town, sir. I'm happy to see you again."

Martin Renahan, the President's House doorman, had occupied the quarters just inside the front door for decades. The old man now stood beside Beede on the north portico and watched with him as the funeral cortege departed.

"And I'm happy to see you, Martin," Beede said. "I'm glad to find that you have remained here despite the change in administration."

"Ah, well, I come highly recommended," Renahan said, with a wry smile. "Both Mr. Van Buren and Mr. Adams vouched for me to old Tippecanoe. It's good to have the benediction of two such distinguished gentlemen."

"I dare say."

"But this . . ." Renahan continued. "'Tis a sad day, indeed. We've not previously had a president die in harness, as they say. Makes for much sadness and a bit of fuss and bother, as well."

"At least it wasn't a lingering illness," Beede said. "I assume he didn't suffer overmuch."

"Indeed," said Renahan. "He might have lived longer, however, had he not received medical attention."

"They bled him?"

"Bled him, cupped him, puked him, and dosed him with calomel, to my certain knowledge," Renahan said. "Who knows what other infernal measures they may have employed in secret."

Beede shrugged. "It is the usual procedure in such cases. Sometimes it just isn't enough."

"And sometimes," Renahan said, "it's far too much. You were at the Battle of New Orleans, with Jackson, were you not?"

"I was."

"Well, then, I leave it to you," he said. "Did you ever see a man die from having too much blood?"

The cortege had moved out of the yard, heading in the direction of the Congressional Cemetery. Beede hurried to catch up. By the time he reached it, the procession was a hundred yards or so down the street.

He followed at a distance for several miles until the funeral party entered the cemetery gates. Beede could hear the Marine Band playing a tune that he did not recognize, perhaps something from the Indian wars that had first brought Harrison to the public eye. It was on the strength of the reputation he had acquired while fighting the Shawnee confederation that Harrison's presidential aspirations had been based. Aside from his Indian-fighting exploits, in fact, Harrison's record in public life had been unremarkable.

The black-draped funeral wagon came to a halt. Harrison's coffin was lifted reverently upon the shoulders of the pallbearers and carried into an empty mausoleum where it would be kept until the weather improved. Beede was familiar with this practice; in New England, cold-weather burials were frequently postponed and bodies held in storage until later in the spring, when the ground had softened sufficiently to take a spade. Ohio winters, Beede thought, must be similar to New England's.

There were no more eulogies or sermons here, and the funeral crowd soon began to disperse. Renahan, who had also followed the procession to the cemetery, fell in step with Beede as they began making their way back to the President's Mansion, which was increasingly referred to as the White House—a name it had received due to the whitewash it had been given after the British had set the building afire during the war.

Washington City had been described as a city of "magnificent intentions." As they walked, Beede was reminded again of the extent to which those intentions fell short of reality. At one end of Pennsylvania Avenue sat the perennially half-finished Capitol building while at the other end the President's House stood surrounded by construction debris. At the president's end of the street, workmen were busily planting rose bushes and other ornamental vegetation. No doubt, Beede thought, the resulting landscape would be attractive when completed; now the putative garden was arid, wallowing in a desert of dust wherever the rain had not turned it to black mud.

"How do you find your new employer, Mr. Tyler?" Beede asked as they walked.

"He ain't my employer," Renahan said, petulantly. "I'm no bloody house nigger, you know. I work for the national government. I'm sort of like a landlord, and Mr. Tyler is merely my present tenant."

"I apologize for my mistake," Beede said. "Is Mr. Tyler easy to work for . . . or, rather, with?"

"So far, yes. Not like General Harrison, with his nightly carousing and his drunken Ohio comrades treating the mansion like it was some cheap frontier tavern."

"Rather more revelry than might be expected from a general, I suppose."

"Quite so. The man was sixty-eight years old, but he seemed to think he was still a twenty-year-old lieutenant. He had guests every night until late. I fancy myself something of a drinker, but I couldn't keep up with old Tippecanoe if I tried."

"Did that hasten his demise, do you think?"

Renahan considered this.

"It might have, indeed," he said after a moment. "He was old when he came here, and not in the best of health. And he was certainly burning the candle at both ends."

Chapter 3

Daniel Webster was known for his skill at entertaining. It was a major part of the duties of secretary of state, and Webster was reputed to be a gracious and amusing host. His company was sought-after, his presence was commanding, and his culinary offerings were highly prized. Women found him attractive. If the truth be told, he enjoyed knowing that women were attracted to him, and he was not immune to their charms. He was a married man, but rumors followed him wherever he went.

This, Beede surmised upon his arrival at Webster's house, would not be one of those festive, convivial evenings.

The house was shuttered, dark, and quiet. Beede could see no sign that the owner of the house was at home, and he wondered briefly if he had miscon-

strued Webster's casual parting remark and had
turned it, in his mind, into an unintended invitation to
dinner. After reviewing the conversation in his mind,
however, he concluded that he had not been mistaken,
that he had, indeed, been invited to dinner to discuss
what Webster had called "a matter of some importance."

This was the date and the time; he was certain of
that. And Webster, Beede thought, did not issue such
invitations frivolously. So, contrary to appearances,
he must be at home.

Beede knocked and was greeted by silence. He
knocked again, to no avail, and was turning to leave
when a voice called to him from around the corner of
the house.

"This way, Mr. Beede," said the voice. Webster's
voice.

Webster was waiting around the corner, where he
led Beede to another door at the rear of the house.

"Please excuse the subterfuge," Webster said when
they had entered and the door had been locked se-
curely behind them. "The matter I wish to discuss is
so delicate that I cannot let it be generally known for
the time being."

He lit a hurricane lamp and led Beede down a narrow corridor. At the end of the corridor, a door opened
into a spacious sitting room. Webster motioned Beede
to a chair and then pulled up another for himself.

"My wife is away, and I've given the servants the
night off," Webster said. "We can talk without inter-
ruption. Our supper will be cold, I fear, but I trust you
will find it satisfactory for all that."

"Is this secrecy really necessary?"

"I believe so," Webster answered. "It is, as I said, a matter of some delicacy."

Beede waited for more, but Webster seemed to be lost in thought.

"And this matter concerns me in some fashion?" Beede ventured when Webster seemed preoccupied.

"I believe so," Webster replied. "The problem, as I'm certain you recognize, is the question of legitimacy. Do we have a president, or do we not? And if so, is it Mr. Tyler?"

"Frankly, Mr. Secretary," said Josiah Beede. "I fear that I do not understand. Your party won the election quite handily."

"But we lost our president, and his successor has taken office under a cloud. This cloud will make Mr. Tyler's effectiveness problematic, at best. He was a compromise choice, who we thought might siphon a few votes from Democrats and strengthen the president's hand a bit. And now, apparently, he is President, a president who is, at heart, antithetical to Whig principles and ideals. Mr. Quincy Adams likes to refer to him as 'His Accidency.' "

"I'd heard that Tyler has been sworn in already."

"True," Webster said. "But should he have been? Was it a legal action? That is the question many people are asking, Senator Clay not least among them. Mr. Clay, as you no doubt know, would like very much to occupy the office of President, and if it is determined that a vacancy exists he will move heaven and earth to secure it for himself."

It occurred to Beede that Henry Clay was not the

only man in America who lusted after the presidency. It was widely believed that Daniel Webster himself had presidential ambitions. They had been swept aside by the Harrison juggernaut, but both men, Beede suspected, continued to nurture their secret aspirations.

"I'm not an authority on the Constitution," Beede said. "Surely you are better situated than I to determine the constitutionality of Mr. Tyler's position."

"I dare say I am," Webster said with a dismissive gesture. "If it were simply a question of whether the actions that have been taken are consistent with the Constitution, I am as knowledgeable as any man in our nation. I am not asking you to interpret the Constitution for me; I require you to determine the facts."

"What facts are these?"

"I must know the manner of General Harrison's death," Webster said. "Did he, as is generally believed, die of a combination of old age, frail health, and some rather foolish behavior on his inauguration day, or is there a more sinister cause?"

"Surely you're not asking if he was murdered!" Beede said in shock.

"That is exactly what I'm asking, sir," Webster replied. "It has been so rumored. I want you to tell me whether he died at the hand of God, or at the rather less charitable hands of another man. If that other man was John Tyler, he cannot be allowed to exercise the duties of the office."

"He exercises those duties now."

"But he must not be allowed to continue . . . if he's guilty of murder."

It took a moment for Beede to absorb the ramifications of such a conjecture. He found it difficult to believe that men would kill for the rather dubious honor of being President. Already in the nation's brief history, presidents had found that the expense of the office outweighed whatever prestige it might bring them, not to mention the bitter criticism and vituperation that had been heaped upon every man who had held the position, from Washington onward.

On the other hand, Harrison had apparently considered the presidency quite an honor, for he had actively campaigned for the position—an unprecedented action that many people had found offensive. But perhaps others had also found it enticing.

"What do you expect me to find?" Beede asked after a moment.

Webster sighed. "I don't know. General Harrison was a hero of the Indian wars, and military heroes often attract enemies, but it's hard to imagine that he attracted much enmity. As military heroes go, I would say he was most ineffectual."

"Can this also be said of his political opinions?"

"Frankly," Webster said, "I was unaware that he had any. He asked me to edit his inaugural remarks, you know. Aside from endeavoring to impress his audience with his classical education—and perhaps to reward them with an hour or so of blessed guilt-free sleep—there was nothing of substance in the text."

"I was unaware that he was trained in the classics," Beede said.

"As was I," Webster said. "But he was enormously proud of it. I killed seventeen Roman proconsuls dead as smelts in the text of his speech. I count that as a public service of some significance."

The meal was surprisingly satisfying. Webster had apparently instructed his servants to lay out an ample supply of cheeses and cold meats. Beede and Webster sat at a table in the kitchen, and the meal was such that, after the first few minutes, the men abandoned attempts at small talk and concentrated on systematically shoveling food into their mouths as quickly as manners permitted. Beede was grateful, for he had very little to say to this man.

"You'll need to speak with some people," Webster said as Beede prepared to leave. "I'll send messages to Mr. Tyler and Mr. Clay that they might expect you. We'll need some sort of cover story; perhaps you can say that you're preparing a eulogy, like nearly everyone else. If you need to speak to someone other than Mr. Clay and Mr. Tyler, I'll see what I can arrange."

"I'll do what I can to investigate," Beede said. "Although your entire premise seems far-fetched to me."

"Do you think so?" Webster said. "You cannot imagine how fervently I wish for you to be proven right."

Chapter 4

On the way back to his lodgings, Beede thought about his curious, clandestine meeting with Webster. Was it possible that General Harrison, the president of the United States, had been murdered? And, if so, why? According to Webster, Harrison had had few political enemies, and his personal life seemed above reproach. And the United States was hardly a world power in the way of England or France or one of the other European nations, where power struggles among heads of state and their pretenders were commonplace.

Moreover, if one were intent upon murdering a president, how could it be done without calling it to the attention of the world? Presidents were not ringed with bodyguards like royalty, but their very accessibility would make the task difficult, if secrecy were the aim. The President's House was a public building, open to visitors. Office seekers roamed the halls at will. People seeking to catch the president's ear were always around, waiting impatiently for an audience. There would be witnesses everywhere.

The trick would be to make his death appear accidental, or at least the result of natural causes, so that no suspicions would be aroused. This, Webster seemed to think, had been accomplished. Beede was less certain, but he resolved to maintain an open mind for the time being.

Poison, he thought, would be the only feasible approach. Arsenic, perhaps. It would take some time, adding the poison to the president's food a little at a time until it had accumulated in the body in lethal dosage levels, but thirty days—the duration of Harrison's short-lived presidency—might have been just long enough. If Harrison had been poisoned, the logical suspects would be those who prepared or served his meals. He should, therefore, question the kitchen staff. Beede knew many of the kitchen workers from his days with Andrew Jackson. He could not imagine any of them committing murder. Nevertheless, he would need to investigate.

Other than the kitchen staff, he supposed, someone with access to the kitchen might also be in a position to poison Harrison's food and drink. In fact, continued exposure to arsenic could have an effect, even if the poison were not ingested.

At his boarding house he climbed the stairs to his room and sprawled on the bed without disrobing. He was tired, but he did not sleep immediately. He drifted off, finally, only an hour or so before the sun flooded his window, reminding him that it was time to arise once more.

The next day was devoted to recreating, in his own mind, the events leading up to Harrison's death. He had, it appeared, died shortly after midnight, surrounded by those friends, family, and colleagues who had arrived with Harrison prior to his inauguration. Death had come quietly, as he slept, although Beede wondered how peaceful the old man could have been, attended by members of Congress, his cabinet, the clerk of the Supreme Court, the mayor, and those members of his family who had accompanied him to Washington. A death watch of sorts had arisen more or less spontaneously in the street outside the mansion, as people waited to hear Harrison's dying words. When he thought about the event, Beede found himself remembering the crowds that had gathered in New Hampshire for the hanging of Jacob Wolf. He hoped that the events surrounding Harrison's death had been a bit less festive than the official execution of a murderer.

I n an outlying village of Warrensboro, New Hampshire, that same morning, Deborah Tomkins Turner awoke slowly in her home and realized that she was alone.

Where was he? Where was her husband?

He had been with her the previous evening; she had fallen asleep beside him. It was still a novel experience, to share her bed with someone who was not a sibling and with no bundling board between them. Not that bundling boards were often employed these days: they were relics of an earlier age when bed space was even scarcer than at present. And now that she was a married woman, of course, it would serve no purpose.

Troubled, she rose and began to search the house. It was not a large house, and it took very little time to determine that he was not there. And not in the barn, either, or the woodlot or the smokehouse. He might be in the privy, she supposed; she would wait for a bit and see if he emerged. In the meantime she would dress herself and coax the banked embers into new life.

She did so, and when the fire was going once more and the previous evening's meal was warming again for breakfast, she sat down to wait. She waited for some time, but he did not return. After a while, she gathered her courage, left the house, and made her way to the privy.

It was unoccupied. She looked into the barn.

"Frank?"

The empty stall told her that his horse was gone.

She felt the first gnawing fear in the pit of her stomach. Wherever her husband had gone, it was, apparently, too far to walk.

Chapter 5

From time to time Josiah Beede found himself wondering at the twists and turns that his life had taken. As a child, and as a young man, he had had no premonitions of greatness—certainly no premonition that he would one day move in the highest circles of the national government. If his father had lived a bit longer, in fact, it was unlikely that he would have found himself in his present position.

Beede had been born in 1801, the youngest of three brothers and the middle of five siblings, to a Massachusetts farmer and his wife. His childhood had been much like those of the children of his neighbors, with sporadic schoolroom instruction interrupted by hard work in the fields. As with most farm families in New England, their farm production had hovered barely above subsistence levels from year to year, but

they had remained basically optimistic. Their produc-
tivity grew every year, and they began to amass some
modest wealth. The future, though unpredictable,
looked pleasant, and Josiah had begun to imagine that
an opportunity for college might even arise. The possibility thrilled him to the core; he enjoyed farm
work—more, perhaps, than his brothers and sisters—
but he had also discovered books. He read widely, vo-
raciously, and the thought of spending several years
of his life in that intensive pursuit was quite attractive.

But it was not to be. His father died and his eldest
brother bought out his siblings' shares of the farm and
offered the younger brothers paid work in the fields at
ludicrously low wages.

Josiah had no particular ambitions and so was content with his situation, but his middle brother, Seth,
seethed with envy. Seth persuaded Josiah that they
should pool their proceeds from the sale and go into
business as itinerant peddlers. They traveled through
the West and the South, ending their journeys in New
Orleans not long before the British invasion in 1815.
And it was there that Josiah became known by General
Andrew Jackson and developed a lifelong association
with the great man.

In New Orleans he met and married a young Creole girl. He read for the law and, upon completion of
his studies, established a practice in the city. When
Jackson was elected President, Beede was called to
Washington City where he served as an important but
unofficial advisor.

His wife died in childbirth, taking their stillborn

son with her. Beede was distraught, but he continued working until he could stand it no more. At that point he closed his now lucrative law practice, resigned from his voluntary service with Jackson, and bought a farm in New England.

That had been more than ten years ago. It had taken half that time to re-establish himself in New England, but he did not regret his decision. He was no longer a stranger now; he was an accepted member of the community. He was, to the extent it was possible, content with his position.

He had remained active in politics, though in a lesser capacity than before, and that interest had frequently brought him back to Washington City to confer with other Democrats concerning the future of the party.

Now he found himself working for his political adversaries, and it was his previous successes that had recommended him for the job at hand. It was, when he thought about it, an astonishing development, and he could not help wondering where his path might take him next.

O n the following morning, Beede went to the President's House and asked to speak to the president. Renahan said he would see what he could do.

Renahan was gone for some time, and Beede grew tired of waiting. Rather than continue standing idly in the foyer, he stepped outside to enjoy the springtime air.

Outside, a small crew of laborers was digging up garden beds, and he stood watching them from the shade of the portico. Five men were planting rose bushes. Three of the men were black, probably—although not necessarily—slaves. One was blond and had been burned pink in the hot spring sunshine. The fifth, apparently the foreman, was a bit lighter than the Negroes who plied the long-handled shovels but not as fair as the other. He was somewhat slighter of build than the others, and apparently much younger, but he seemed to be in charge. He was beardless, with restless dark eyes and a manner of moving that reminded Beede of a cat: smooth and purposeful, with little wasted motion. He was shirtless like the others, with a muscular frame that indicated the presence of controlled energy just below the surface. He had an easy grin, and his colleagues seemed to follow his directives without resentment, despite his youth.

The younger man was also aware of his surroundings in a way the others did not seem to be, and inevitably he noticed Beede watching him. He straightened from his labors, brushed the loam from his hands, and sauntered over to where Beede stood.

"Good morning, sir. Isn't it a beautiful day?"

"Indeed," Beede replied. "And these roses will make the days more beautiful, I believe. They will certainly brighten the President's House immensely."

"That's the idea," said the young man. "It's the reason I was hired, after all. I believe I employ the finest gardening staff in a hundred miles or more. The President's House should have the best. And I am the best in this business." There were black marks on his hand, which Beede at first assumed to be dirt clods but ultimately realized were lesions or scars of a sort.

"I must take your word for that."

"That isn't necessary. Ask around at all the elegant houses in Washington City, or even Baltimore; they'll all tell you: if you're looking for beauty and elegance, you can't do better than Charles Panther. Remember me when you decide to beautify your dwellings."

"Unfortunately, I live elsewhere. In New England."

"And I don't work so far away as that," said Panther. "Nevertheless, remember my name. If your fortunes change in the future, and you find yourself back in Washington City, you may well need my services."

"I'll certainly keep you in mind," Beede said. He was about to say more when Renahan appeared to say that the president was now free to speak with him.

"**M**urdered!" said John Tyler. "General Harrison was not murdered! The very idea is absurd!"

"I daresay you are correct," Beede said. "But it has never happened before that a president has died in office, and suspicions are bound to arise. Mr. Webster has charged me with the duty of laying those suspicions to rest."

"I understand his concern," said Tyler, "but his fears are unfounded. The general's death stemmed from natural causes. Entirely."

"You're certain of this?"

"He died of pleurisy and foolishness," Tyler said. "His illness was the direct result of overexposure during a formidable winter storm. He was an old man, and he did not take proper care of himself."

"How so?"

Tyler gestured impatiently. "Please take a seat, sir. We can discuss this matter more comfortably if we are seated."

He hardly waited for Beede to settle into the wooden chair by the fireplace before launching into his monologue.

"General Harrison was sixty-eight years old when he died," Tyler said. "He was desperately afraid—owing to his advanced age—that people would consider him too old for the rigors of public office, in particular for the highest elected public office in the land. The sad fact is that he *was* too old and too ill for the job, but he went to great effort to disguise this fact. He spoke at great length out of doors at his inauguration; he rode bareheaded in the wind and rain through the streets of the city; he stayed up late most evenings, playing cards, drinking, and joking with his companions. I hesitate to speak ill of the man, but he was, in many respects, his own worst enemy."

"I had heard that," Beede said.

"And did you hear how he spent his inaugural day?" Tyler asked. "There were inaugural balls all over the city, and he attended all of them. He could have hired a carriage, but he elected instead to ride on horseback—bareheaded, again, through the rain and the cold—to each affair. He had no regard for his health, and I venture to say little regard for his country, else he would have been more prudent."

"I am reluctant to ask this," Beede said, "but it

would be helpful to know where you were when he died."

"Surely you do not suspect me of harming the old man?"

"I do not," Beede said. "But for my report I should do my best to eliminate any potential suspects, and you were next in line for the office."

"Very well. I was at home."

"At home? In Washington?"

"In Williamsburg," Tyler said. "I was vice president, which, as you know, is a position akin to that of a bride on her wedding night, awaiting the arrival of her husband. Once the ceremonial proceedings are completed, she has no role to play until she is called upon."

"My wife was in poor health," Tyler continued, "and I felt that my duty was to be with her. I did not anticipate being called upon in my vice presidential capacity in the near future. Indeed, I did not expect to be called upon *at all* during General Harrison's four years in office. If the president lives, there is no need for a vice president."

"How did you learn of the president's death?"

"Dan Webster sent his son to inform me. Young Fletcher traveled all night and appeared at my door early the next morning. After hearing his mournful news I left for Washington City that same day."

"Were you on good terms with General Harrison?"

"Reasonably so, I believe," Tyler said. "I didn't know him well. We were both born on James River plantations, almost within earshot of each other, but our lives took quite different paths. He went to

Hampden-Sydney and I to William and Mary. Then I returned to Virginia, and he went on to the western territories. And you must recall that he was considerably older than I. We had little in common beyond our birthplace."

"You were both slaveholders, I believe," Beede said.

"Yes, you're correct," Tyler said. "But that's hardly a point of distinction. All Virginians of quality own slaves."

Tyler stood suddenly and made a show of glancing at the clock in the corner.

"I regret, sir, that I have no more time to spare for you this morning," he said. "Martin will show you out."

"So what's your impression of my President?" Renahan asked as they stepped onto the portico.

"He's congenial enough, I suppose."

"He is that," Renahan agreed. "I shouldn't say this, I guess, but he's much more to my liking than the old general. Reminds me a bit of General Jackson."

"He's long and lanky, like Jackson," Beede admitted. "Not as smart, I'd say."

"I'll give you that, also," Renahan replied. "But he knows what he's about. Senator Clay thinks he can run the country from down the street at the Capitol and render Mr. Tyler irrelevant, but I think he's in for a rude awakening."

•   •   •

Beede spent the remainder of the day calling upon friends and political acquaintances, not really expecting to find anyone who shared Webster's suspicions. In this respect, however, he was surprised. It seemed to be commonly accepted wisdom that the old general had received a helping hand on his journey to the Great Beyond. Not everyone he consulted shared Webster's suspicions, but there were enough who did to cause Beede to begin to consider the possibility more seriously.

"He was old, it's true, and not in the best of health," said a military veteran of Beede's acquaintance, expressing a view he heard repeatedly. "But he was a tough old bird. After surviving the battles at Tippecanoe and the Thames, it's inconceivable that he would die of pleurisy, or whatever they say he died from."

"Could he have been poisoned, do you think?"

The veteran shrugged. "Anything's possible, I suppose," he said.

"But you don't believe it?"

"As I said, anything's possible, but it's hard to imagine a motive. What did General Harrison ever do to anybody that they should want to murder him? I just can't see it."

Beede retired to his lodgings at the end of the day, no wiser or more knowledgeable than when he had begun.

For the next several days he continued his quest, seeking all those who might be knowledgeable about Harrison's final days on earth, but he was unable to come to a conclusion with which he felt comfortable.

There were those who suspected foul play, and there were those who did not, but they could marshal little evidence for either position. The reality continued to lie just outside his reach, and he found the situation frustrating in the extreme.

He returned to his lodgings one evening, a week after he had begun his investigation, to find a letter awaiting him. Recognizing the neat handwriting, he took the letter quickly to his room and hastily broke the seal.

The letter, as he had surmised, was from Deborah Tomkins.

"I hesitate to intrude upon your concerns," she had written, "but I do not know where else to turn. It is an embarrassing matter, and I require the assistance of someone whose sense of discretion is indisputable. My husband appears to have left me."

Beede read the letter through, then put it aside and thought. Then he read it again, more carefully, seeking whatever meaning might lie hidden between the words on the page.

Again he put the letter aside and stared out the window of his room at the stable yard below. He stared at the yard, not quite seeing it, and thought for some time.

Chapter 6

On the afternoon of October 12, in the year 1840, Deborah Tomkins had been wed in a simple ceremony in the parlor of the Tomkins home in Warrensboro, New Hampshire. It was a small ceremony, but it was well attended by residents of the community, not only out of goodwill toward the bride and groom but also out of respect for the bride's father, easily the wealthiest and most influential man in town.

Josiah Beede, unfortunately, was unable to be present. Court had resumed in Concord, the state capital, and his services had been required there. He performed his duties with half a mind and half his heart and hurried back to Warrensboro as soon as he could decently do so.

Privately, Beede was devastated by this develop-

ment, although he tried not to show it. He had
thought, and had believed that Deborah had also
thought, that she would readily have assented to their
marriage—if only he had asked. But he had not
asked, and another man had.

Deborah's father agreed with Beede's assessment
when the two met at a local tavern not long before
Beede had left for Concord and the court.

"I really thought I would be welcoming you to the
family," said old Israel Tomkins, pulling deeply on
his clay pipe. "In fact, I had been looking forward to
it. I had had some doubts about you, I must admit,
when you first settled in Warrensboro, but I came to
believe that you were a valuable addition to our community. I came to believe, also, that you and Deborah
were well matched."

"I had reached a similar conclusion," Beede said,
ruefully. "It is embarrassing to discover that I had so
misjudged the situation."

"I'm not certain that you misjudged the situation
at all," Tomkins said. "It's my belief that you merely
failed to act on your conclusions in a timely manner,
and Deborah grew tired of waiting. There was, perhaps, an element of desperation in her decision as
well."

"Deborah need not have felt desperation," Beede
said. "I cannot conceive of Deborah as a spinster, and
surely it was clear that I was enamored of her."

"And how had you made this clear?" Tomkins
said. "Not through any outward show of affection,
certainly. And not by word, either."

It had grown unaccountably warm for autumn,

and the fire that usually roared in the taproom had been allowed to die down. Beede was, nevertheless, feeling chilled.

"It's one thing to tell yourself that you needn't be too eager and snap up the first suitor who comes around," Tomkins continued. "I don't doubt that she's aware of that. But it's more difficult to spurn potential suitors when you receive no encouragement from the one you would prefer. You've been away so much, between your legal business and your political concerns, that Deborah apparently concluded that you were not available. However much I may regret her decision to marry, I must say I can't argue with it."

"I had intended to pay a call to her as soon as I was free to do so," Beede protested. "I had expected to be free of my obligations before now."

"In the absence of some word from you," Tomkins said mildly, "how could she have known that?"

Beede knew that the old man was right. Duty had ever exercised a call on his services, and the call had often come at inconvenient moments. So it had been before; so had it been in this instance, and he had been the loser.

Beede did what he could to adapt to his new situation. Not long after his return to Warrensboro he made it a point to call upon the new couple. Deborah had married Franklin Turner, an established husbandman in the nearby village of West Warrensboro. He was nearly as old as Beede, and in possession of a considerable portion of land and a position of hard-won influence in the community.

Despite Beede's misgivings, he had been received warmly when he called upon the couple. The awkwardness he had anticipated did not come about. Husband and wife both greeted him unreservedly; Turner returned from the fields to welcome him.

"Do not concern yourself about it," Turner said when Beede apologized for taking him from his chores. "I've little enough to do at this time of year, as you're no doubt aware. And Deborah has told me so much about you that I've been hoping for an opportunity to meet you. You're the subject of much discussion, you know, even here in West Warrensboro. It's all favorable, of course."

Deborah, Beede noted, smiled and blushed at her husband's remarks. Beede found it most becoming.

"Very kind of you, sir." Beede said.

"Nothing of the sort. I'm simply stating a well-established fact. Your admirers are legion, sir. You are the Boy Hero of New Orleans!"

"Never a hero," Beede replied. "And no longer a boy."

Beede had never learned how to deal with the public perception that he was a hero, which he knew to be false, or at least an exaggeration. On the field of battle at Chalmette Plantation, he had reacted out of an overwhelming sense of guilt at the death of his brother, whose life had been taken by a British musket ball during the thirty-minute conflict outside the city of New Orleans. The grief and guilt was fueled by Beede's own certain knowledge that Seth's death was his responsibility: Beede had frozen in fear at the awesome sight of the ranks of British regulars advancing on their position behind a makeshift bulwark of river clay and cotton bales. Seth had attempted to pull Beede to safety, but the bullet, which had probably been meant for Beede, took his brother's life instead.

In grief and fury Beede had picked up a nearby rifle—one that its dead owner had had no further use for—and had begun firing blindly toward the enemy. It was that rage that had caught the eye of Andrew Jackson and had cemented his reputation as a war hero.

It was a reputation that Beede was acutely aware that he did not deserve and had not earned, but it had remained with him all his life. After a while he had given up the attempt to set the record straight. In truth, the reputation had opened doors for him. Jackson had taken him under his wing—Beede was only fifteen at the time—and others had taken his reputation at face value, throughout his years reading for the law and practicing the law and serving as an advisor to Jackson during his presidency. Even Adrienne Dumond, the young Creole girl whom he had married and later lost to childbed fever, had been impressed as much by his reputation as by his person.

Before she died, taking their stillborn son with her, she had come to see Beede in a different, less favorable light. As much as anything else in his life, Beede regretted that he would have no opportunity to restore her faith in him, or her love.

With Deborah he had thought there might be a chance to make amends for his previous shortcomings. He now realized that it was not to be. He had hesitated, and he had lost, and Deborah had married another.

Sitting now in her husband's house, the guilt returned full force, accompanied by an unaccustomed sense of self-pity. He forced that feeling away, knowing it to be dishonorable and unproductive, but he knew also that it lay waiting for him just out of reach and would return in some unguarded moment.

The conversation went on for an hour or so, until Beede felt he should make his manners and depart. Turner shook his hand firmly at the door and Deborah smiled brightly. He left with their farewells in his ears and a hollow space in his heart.

Chapter 7

Beede had never doubted that he would heed Deborah's request. He had given dutiful consideration to the task Webster had set for him, but his mind returned repeatedly to the letter that had come from Deborah Tomkins in New Hampshire. He puzzled over what it might mean but could not reach a conclusion—which meant, in all likelihood, that the answers could only be found at home.

Webster, as Beede had anticipated, was unhappy.

"May I inquire as to the nature of this sudden emergency?" he asked. "Is it so important that you must break off an important investigation on which the future of this nation so depends?"

"I believe so," Beede said. "I will not know for certain until I have investigated on my own. My correspondent certainly feels it to be so."

"And who is your . . . no, I will not ask. I will take you at your word in this matter. Will you at least promise to return once the problem in New Hampshire is resolved? I must assume the situation here will keep for a little while."

"It might even be resolved on its own in that time," Beede said. "But yes, if it's necessary, I'll return."

"Then go," Webster said, grudgingly. "But hurry back. I have a premonition that all here is not as it seems."

The journey back to Warrensboro seemed amazingly fast, particularly when compared to his previous trips from Washington by horse and stagecoach. There was railroad service now, which greatly reduced the time in transit, though at a considerable cost both to his pocketbook and to his soot-tarnished clothing. On the second day of his journey Beede was able to redeem his little Morgan horse from the stable in Concord where he had boarded him, and begin the brief ride to his farm, fifteen miles away.

He took the turnpike and rode fast. As a rule he preferred to avoid the toll road and to travel at a more leisurely pace, but there had been an undercurrent of urgency in Deborah's letter that seemed to warrant a bit of speed.

He came upon his own farm first and was pleased to see that everything was in order, that Randolph had seen to the hiring of itinerant labor to prepare the soil and plant crops. Beede had left some money behind to pay for labor and to compensate Randolph for the time he had to spend away from his own plantings. He wondered how the hired hands had reacted to the idea of working for a colored man. If past experience was any indication, it had probably been a difficult period of adjustment.

Randolph's farm was adjacent to Beede's, so Beede kept riding past his gateyard and pulled up at the next house. As he was tying his horse to a porch railing, Randolph's door banged open. Beede looked up to see Randolph's wife, Louisa, beaming at him.

"Thought that was you," she said. "Please come in."

"I can only stay a minute or so," Beede said. "I've come back on urgent business."

"I know. Deborah tol' me 'bout her troubles," Louisa said. "Fact is, I'm the one said she should write to you. She's just about at her wit's end from worryin'."

"What happened? Her letter was rather cryptic. Has her husband abandoned her?"

"Don't nobody know," she said with a shrug. "Leastwise not me. I'll let her tell you what she can. That way, you gets it straight."

"Perhaps I should move along, then, and go visit her at her farm."

"No need," she said. "She ain't there; she moved back in with her papa and mama. She couldn't run that ol' farm by herself. I sent Randolph out to the Tomkins place just now to tell her you was here and to invite her to have supper with us. She'll be along directly, I expect."

Beede took the opportunity to conduct a brief inspection of Randolph's property and was pleasantly surprised at the changes that had been wrought. Jacob Wolf, the previous owner, had been old and in poor health for many years, and the farm had suffered considerably from neglect. Fortunately, Randolph had thrown himself into the work at hand, and the property had been considerably improved. There had been holes in the farmhouse roof when Beede had last visited, but there were none now. Wolf had, understandably, been reluctant to ascend to the roof to attend to the repairs; Randolph had not.

Randolph was the first to arrive. He greeted Beede enthusiastically, which eased Beede's mind considerably. The two men had not seen or communicated with each other for several months.

"Deborah will be along shortly," Randolph said. "She was engaged in clothes washing for the family and felt that she could not stop."

"Your farm is doing well," Randolph said. "I hired a young Irishman, who in turn employed two other young Irishmen to assist him. They're all fast learners, and they put things in order rather quickly. If you're looking for tenants to continue running things in your absence, you could do worse than to keep them on."

"It's my hope—and my heartfelt wish—that my days of absence from the farm will soon be behind me," Beede said. "When I retired from Washington it was with the intention of living out the remainder of my life here. Instead, I find myself being pulled in a dozen different directions, and my absences grow longer and more frequent."

"That, sir, is your fate," Randolph said. "You might as well resign yourself to that. Your reputation precedes you."

"And how do you fare?" Beede asked. "Is Louisa treating you well? And little Nancy?"

"We have our rough patches yet, Louisa and I," Randolph said. "But I can't complain. We're growing more comfortable with each other every day. Nancy makes everything easier."

"You don't find it difficult to accept her, knowing that she's another man's daughter?"

"That's the surprising thing," Randolph said with a laugh. "I had feared that I might. I had thought that I might find her very existence offensive, an omnipresent reminder of the overseer who took advantage of Louisa in my absence. It hasn't happened, however. I think it would have been harder had she been a boy, but she looks so much like Louisa that most days I don't even think about the overseer. And Nancy dotes on me in a way that Louisa never has— or ever will."

"Have you been back to the meeting house for Sabbath services?"

"Once or twice," Randolph said. "Louisa wanted to go. I fancy she thought it would help her adjust to being free."

"And did it?"

Randolph shrugged. "We were not attacked, verbally or physically, but it was far from a pleasant experience. The congregation didn't welcome us with open arms, and Pastor Gray stared openly at us from the pulpit."

Louisa appeared in the doorway.

"Miz Turner has arrived," she said.

Beede had seen Deborah Tomkins—now Deborah
Tomkins Turner—many times in many different circumstances, but her appearance this day was unlike
any he had experienced before. She possessed the
same regular features as in the past, but her blue eyes
were red from weeping, and her countenance was
grave, indeed. Upon entering the room she spied him
and crossed quickly to his side. It was as if they had
been husband and wife for many years, rather than
merely neighbors and acquaintances.

He held her, awkwardly, as she burrowed her face
in his chest and sobbed quietly for a time. Eventually
she disengaged herself and stepped back, wiping her
eyes as she did so.

"I'm sorry for my behavior, Mr. Beede. Whatever
must you think of me?"

"I think of you as a mature young woman who has
undergone a severe ordeal," Beede said consolingly.
"I do not judge you or think less of you because of it.
Truth to tell, I share your anguish."

"Thank you for your kindness and understanding,"
she said, still wiping her eyes.

"Come sit by me and tell me your story," Beede
said, motioning to a window seat big enough for the
two of them. She joined him at the window and sat
beside him.

"Now tell me what you can," he said. "As thoroughly as possible."

The floodgates opened. Amid a torrent of tears,
Deborah told Beede about her husband's disappear-

ance. It was clearly a difficult topic for her, and the story was interrupted frequently for another spate of crying.

She told Beede about falling asleep beside her husband only to awaken early and find him gone. He had said nothing about going away, she said, and so she had come slowly to the realization that she was alone in the house.

"Do you have any thoughts as to where he might have gone?" Beede asked.

"No, nor why," she replied. "I was all unknowing, and I remain so. He seemed content. There was no great passion in our marriage, but neither was there contempt or disdain. We were comfortable with each other."

"That is important," Beede said. From his marriage to Adrienne Dumond, Beede knew well that passion could turn to contempt over the years. He was inclined to believe that comfort would serve Deborah better than passion. And although he hated himself for feeling so, he experienced a feeling of sadness and loss at the realization.

"And was there no note, no letter, to inform you of his whereabouts?" he asked. "Nothing to alleviate your natural fears?"

"Nothing," she said.

"And this has never happened before?"

"Never."

"Strange," said Beede. "Is there anything else that you can tell me? Anything that might indicate where he might have gone . . . or why?"

"Only that he took his horse. To me, that indicates

a journey of some distance—more than a few miles. And he has been gone now for a week."

"Strange," Beede said, again. "Perhaps I should visit your farm. I don't know that I can discover anything that you haven't noticed, but . . ."

"Oh, please, sir," Deborah said. "I would be most grateful."

"I'll leave in the morning," he said. "I'd be pleased if you could accompany me. Perhaps you'll see something you missed previously."

"If I must," she said. "I do not look forward to returning there."

"I would find it helpful. If something is out of the ordinary, you would be more apt to notice it than I."

"Why don't y'all stay here tonight?" Louisa said. "You'll be that much closer to where you be goin' if you stay with us, and you can get an early start in the mornin'."

"I hesitate to impose on you," Beede said. "My farm is nearby, after all. I can sleep there tonight."

"Your house is filled with them Irishmen that been workin' your fields," Louisa said. "Meanin' no disrespect, sir, but you just be in the way over there. We can find room for you here, Miz Turner, too. It's closer than goin' back to her house.

"Don't be silly, sir," she said when Beede hesitated. "It ain't no bother for me. I'll be pleased to have some guests—makes me feel more like a real free woman. I been here three years. It's about time I had some guests."

•   •   •

Beede and Randolph remained after the rest of the household had gone to bed. They sat staring at the dying hearth fire, each lost in thought. For his part, Beede thought of his two dissimilar puzzles: the fate of Frank Turner and the cause of President Harrison's death.

He had little faith in his ability to find an answer to either mystery. Whatever reputation he had gained as a sleuth—which apparently was considerable—had come about by happenstance. He had no particular skills, and no particular method, for unraveling such a tangled skein as this. Frank Turner had lived in the next village for many years, but Beede felt he knew even less about him than about the late President Harrison.

"What do you know about Deborah's husband?" he said at last.

"Very little," Randolph replied. "I met him once, when Deborah brought him by for an introduction not long after they were wed. We were not invited to the wedding, of course. I'm treated better here than in the South, but it's made clear to me each day that I'm not an equal."

"What was your impression of him?"

"Oh, he was polite enough," Randolph said. "Polite but condescending. He spoke to me respectfully but managed to convey the sense that I was a small child—and not a very bright one. He seemed to feel that he had to explain any big words to me, as if I had never heard them before. If I hadn't known that he was born in Massachusetts, I'd have thought him a southerner."

"That can't be a unique experience. You've been patronized before, both in the North and in the South."

"Certainly. But he grew especially tiresome after a time. He was a colonizer. He believes in removing Negroes to Africa and establishing a colony for us there. He seemed perturbed that I could not be persuaded to join the first wave of immigrants. I told him that I had not been to Africa—that it was as foreign to me as it would be to him—and that it held no allure for me whatsoever. He took that with considerable discontent."

"I can see your point," Beede said. "Nevertheless, I should think that colonization might be attractive to some people of color."

"Perhaps . . . to a slave who has no other options. I have a wife, a child, a farm of my own, and my freedom. Why should I throw all that away in return to begin anew halfway around the world in a place I do not know?"

"Reasonable objections," Beede said. "Then I suppose he should go south and appeal to slaves."

"I suggested that," Randolph said. "He was conspicuously unresponsive to the idea. He would have to buy slaves from their masters—or steal them—and neither approach appealed to him. I believe he was less interested in ridding the country of slavery than he was in ridding the country of Negroes."

"That hardly sounds like a man whom Deborah would marry," Beede said.

"I agree," said Randolph. "Doubtless she was unaware of these sentiments at the time. It isn't the sort of thing a man might discuss with his betrothed, under ordinary circumstances."

Chapter 8

The ride to the Turner farm took almost two hours the following morning, although the distance was only a little over five miles. They had borrowed the carriage belonging to Israel Tomkins, Deborah's father, and had hooked up Beede's Morgan horse to carry them. But it was April, and the mud of springtime made travel difficult. A month earlier, Beede thought ruefully, they could have traveled speedily and in relative comfort by sleigh. There were still patches of snow on the ground in the shaded areas by the roadside even now, but they had been worn off the roads by sunlight and wagon wheels.

Beede had expected to find the farm deserted and fallen into disrepair. He was surprised to see cattle in the fields and livestock in the farmyard. He said as much to Deborah.

"My father hired one of my neighbors to feed the animals since they cannot fend for themselves," she said. "The neighbor also comes for the milking and to gather the eggs, for I cannot use them if I'm not living here. You'll notice, though, that no planting has begun. If Frank does not return soon, no planting *will* be done."

Beede tied his Morgan to a porch railing and helped Deborah down from the carriage. He took a stroll around the farmyard to search for signs of occupancy. Deborah entered the house; he could hear her moving from room to room. As in most New England farmhouses, there were not many rooms to search, and she returned quickly from her investigation.

"Nothing."

"Could you determine whether he might have returned since you departed?" Beede asked. "Perhaps he came back after you left and was disheartened to find that you were gone."

"If he returned, he left no sign of it," she said. "His hat remains on the peg where he had left it, and he hasn't been into the larder, I don't believe."

"Let us check out the barn," Beede said. "And perhaps the fields."

The barn was empty; save for the remains of the previous winter's forage, it appeared to be untouched. This was surprising, Beede thought. During the winter most farmers devoted considerable time to repairing their implements in anticipation of the upcoming planting season. Beede could see both a hoe and a scythe standing against a wall, and both were in need of the services of a blacksmith. The plow, sitting idly nearby, was in better condition, but a harness was hanging on the wall, and it clearly required mending before it could be used. Beede wondered whether Turner had allowed his farm to deteriorate to such a degree in previous years, and if so, how he had come by his reputation for diligence.

The fields had, at least, been cut for forage, but the cut grasses had been left on the ground rather than collected for storage in the hayloft. It was now too late to salvage most of it, which meant that Turner would be forced to rely on cooperative neighbors, willing to sell him their excess. It could be found, Beede supposed, but the price would be dear.

They returned disconsolately to Warrensboro where Beede met with Deborah's father, Israel Tomkins, and explained that the situation on the Turner farm was dire. Tomkins immediately arranged for a few neighbors to pitch in with the task of putting the farm to rights. Beede joined them, as did Randolph, and in a few days the state of affairs had improved to the point that Deborah might be able to return, with hired help, and make the farm functional again.

Beede accompanied her on her return trip. On the journey she sat silently beside him, staring pensively ahead. Beede wondered if she were having second thoughts about her decision to marry. He wondered about the decision himself, not entirely because of his own loss.

Suddenly, as they approached the farmhouse, Deborah stood and shouted.

"Stop, Mr. Beede! Please stop!"

Beede followed her gaze to a corner of the field and saw immediately what had caught her attention. The field had been left fallow, but it had not been undisturbed. Ground had been broken in a far corner and then hastily covered over.

Telling Deborah to remain with the carriage, Beede crossed the soft ground to the digging site. The excavation was recent, he realized. Had Turner begun planting before his disappearance? If so, why had he started here? And why had he abandoned his task?

"What is it?" he heard Deborah ask. As he had feared, she had not remained with the carriage.

"This is not the work of a plow," Beede said. "Rather the blade of a shovel."

He scuffed the broken soil and felt something solid, but yielding, underneath the surface. With a premonition of disaster he turned to persuade Deborah to return to the carriage, but it was too late. She had moved around Beede probing the earth herself, and her foot uncovered what could only be a human hand.

"I recognize that ring," she said, pointing to an exposed finger. "This is Frank! This is my husband!"

Chapter 9

Deborah had returned to the Tomkins farm, and Constable Stephen Huff had been called. He had come quickly, joining Beede in the far corner of the field, to help unearth the body.

"There's no doubt that this is Frank Turner," said Constable Huff. "How long you figure he's been here? About a week?"

"That's what Deborah thinks," Beede said. "He's been in the ground a little while, so it's difficult to determine when he died."

"He took a bad clout to the back of the head, looks like," Huff said. "You see, I'm learning from you. Never would have figured that out if I hadn't seen you work."

"You might never have needed to know this kind of thing if I hadn't come to Warrensboro," Beede said. "Violence and murder seem to follow me around."

"I think we just better get used to the fact that this sort of thing is getting more common all the time," said Huff. "The world just gets rougher and meaner every day. Nothing to do with you at all."

"That's some comfort, I suppose," Beede said. "Though it's a form of comfort I'd as soon do without."

"Well, there ain't nothing we can do about that," Huff said. "What do you suppose he got hit with? Shovel or somethin'?"

"It very well might have been a shovel. Something flat and wide and heavy, in any event. I don't see anything around here that might have served as a murder weapon, though."

Beede and Huff had worked comfortably together when investigating the murder of a mill girl, several years earlier, and had come to a mutual respect. They moved in different circles, however, and saw each other only rarely. Huff lived near the tavern in the village center, while Beede's farmhouse stood a few miles south of the village.

Huff stood and looked around in all directions, shrugged, and once more squatted on the ground beside Beede.

"Thought maybe there might be some sort of clue right nearby," he said in response to Beede's curious glance. "Frank Turner's a peaceable man, but I don't think he'd come out here to be murdered of his own inclination."

"I doubt that he was expecting to be killed," Beede

replied. "I see no signs that he struggled against his assailant, and the damaged area is on the back of his head. He probably was struck unawares."

"Meaning he did not see the blow that killed him," said Huff with a nod. "I suppose that's a reasonable supposition."

"We'll know more when we find the murder weapon."

"If we find it," Huff said, rising once more. "Shall we inspect the barn, then?"

Neither man expected to find a bloody shovel in the barn, and, indeed, they did not. In fact, they found no shovel at all, which struck both men as curious. Shovels were common, and necessary, implements on a farm.

"Should we assume, do you suppose, that the murderer took it away with him?" Huff asked.

"Let us make no assumptions at this time," Beede said. "We have several acres yet to inspect."

But three hours of concentrated searching yielded no results, and the two eventually called a halt. Although the days were growing longer again as spring approached, dusk still began its approach by late afternoon, and it became much more difficult to see what they were doing.

"Should we return again tomorrow?" Huff said as they made their farewells. "I confess that I'm growing discouraged."

"I, too," Beede said. "Yet I think that tomorrow we should finish what we have begun. If we find the shovel tomorrow, we'll be better off than we were. And if we do not, we're no worse situated. There isn't a lot of ground left to cover, however, and we should be able to finish the job tomorrow."

They parted company and left in different directions, each to his respective destination: Huff to his own home and Beede to Randolph's.

As he made his way back, however, something continued to nag at his mind. Some discrepancy—something missing or, at least, out of place—called to him, demanding his attention. But it lingered just out of reach, no matter how hard he groped for it.

It came to him, as he was raising the latch on Randolph's gate, that they still hadn't found Turner's horse, or accounted for it. Deborah had assumed that Turner took it with him when he left the farm. Now, it appeared, Turner had not left the farm at all.

So where was the horse? Was it possible that, when they found the horse, they would also find Turner's murderer?

It was something to think about, and Beede thought about it until he fell asleep that evening.

Chapter 10

The following morning, Beede rode his Morgan horse to the village, as much to exercise his horse as for any other reason. Normally, Peter would be employed in the fields at this time of year and would be worked hard. But this year, with his farm contracted to hired men, Beede had little hard work to perform, and his horse had less.

As he rode into town he noted subtle changes in the village landscape. Previously fallow fields had been cultivated, and several new fields had been cleared. A new roof had been installed on the schoolhouse. Local roads had been marginally improved with better gradients that helped channel rainwater away from the roadbed and into drainage ditches alongside.

One of the things that had first attracted him to

Warrensboro when he decided to leave Washington City and return to New England, was the sense that here was an industrious community whose inhabitants were not afraid of work that improved the common lot. There were not so very many such communities; New England and its rural residents had a reputation for slovenliness that was known throughout the country. Everywhere a traveler went in New England he saw farmhouses with leaking roofs, broken fences, decrepit rock walls, and cluttered barnyards. Village greens were green no longer and were cluttered more with trash and rotting lumber than with sheep.

Beede understood how difficult it was to stay ahead of the necessary chores. More than once he had cut his workday short of his objective in order to catch up on some much-needed rest. But Warrensboro, due no doubt in no small measure to the conscientious example set by old Israel Tomkins, stood as an ever-present reminder of the benefits of honest work, diligently performed.

He decided that it would be appropriate to pay a visit to the Tomkins family and maneuvered his horse in that direction. As he passed Skinner's store, however, a high-pitched musical voice called his name.

It was Mercy, Pastor Gray's eldest child. She stood on the porch—in the South they would have called it a verandah—and waved to him as he rode by. She signaled to him to stop and chat.

"I had no idea you were back in town," she said. "I had heard you were in Washington City on some sort of legal business. It's so good that you have returned to us."

The gushing tone in her voice, which he had once found attractive, even flattering, had begun to wear on his nerves. He remembered a painful evening at the Grays' parsonage with Mercy's mother and father foisting her upon him, the eligible neighbor, and insisting that she favor him with a concert of fiddle tunes that she had learned. It had been a painful—indeed an excruciating—evening and he had promised himself not to be trapped in another such experience.

"Good afternoon, Miss Gray," he said, with a tip of his hat.

"Oh, goodness," she said with a laugh. "I'm not someone's maiden aunt. Please call me Mercy. Let's don't stand on ceremony; you're much too young to be a father figure to me."

"Very well . . . um . . . Mercy. So how are you this evening?"

"Happy to see you, Josiah. May I call you Josiah? I've wanted to be on more comfortable terms with you for ever so long."

"Certainly."

"Oh, thank you!" she said. Was she mocking him? Probably so, he thought. Young women were always mocking him, as if they knew things about him that he did not know about himself. This knowledge did not please him, but he had become reconciled to it.

"Have you returned to us for a prolonged period, or is Warrensboro merely a way station on your journeys?" she was asking.

"This is my home now, Miss . . . Mercy. I leave only when I must in order to tend to my affairs."

"I know," she said. "I know." She made a pretty little pout. "But you are in such demand, by so many, and in so many places. How do you cope with the demands of your farm while also tending to the business of the public?"

"I fear my farm has languished," he said. It was true. During the past two years, even before his journey to New Orleans to help Randolph release Louisa from slavery, he had been forced to contract with a series of itinerant laborers to manage his agricultural activities. "It is in the hands of hired men at present, but I hope to return to it soon."

"See that you do so," she said with feigned severity. "Your absence makes it difficult for young ladies."

"I fear I am not yet free of my responsibilities," Beede said, making ready to go. "I am obliged to help Deborah Turner find her husband. He has disappeared."

"I heard about that," she said. "Poor Deborah. Well, I shall not keep you from your duties, but promise me that you will call on me before you take leave of the community once more. I look forward to visiting with you again."

When he reached the Tomkins farm he found that Huff had arrived before him. He joined Huff and Deborah in conversation in a small gazebo behind the house. Her father, Deborah said, was in Concord tending to state business.

Beede brought up the subject of Turner's missing horse. Deborah said she had no idea what had happened to it.

"It concerned me at times that Frank took such care with that horse," Deborah was saying. "He took no such pains with his cattle, which provide us with milk and meat, for example. But I suppose men have much closer relationships with their horses."

"We don't ride our cattle," Huff pointed out. "A horse can help us on the farm and then take us to Sabbath meeting. It's much more useful than a cow, or a steer."

"And yet," Deborah said, "what is an ox except a big steer? We once depended on our oxen as much as we now depend on horses, but I doubt you ever cared for your oxen as diligently as you do your horse."

"It's hard to have a conversation with an ox the way you can with a horse," said Huff. "I sometimes feel that my horse understands what I am telling her, but my ox—when I had an ox—was oblivious."

"May we now return to our original topic?" Beede asked. "I was inquiring about Mr. Turner's horse. Could it have escaped the barn and wandered off, or was it more likely stolen?"

"Stolen," said Huff. "I'd stake my life on it. Doubtless the murderer took it to effect his escape."

Beede looked at Deborah. "Did you hear someone in the barn that night?"

"I thought it was Frank," she said with a nod. "After all, who else would be in our barn after dark?"

"You did not investigate?"

"I did not. I had had a long day," she said. "I did not get out of bed. In fact, I was barely awake." She gave them an awkward, shamefaced smile. "I am new to the duties of a wife, I fear, and the work is more than I had anticipated. I've seen my mother work, and, of course, I have helped her with her chores, but it's quite another thing to be responsible for it—for all of it—alone."

"Did Frank come to bed at all?"

"I believe he did. The bedclothes had been disturbed on his side of the bed. I cannot confirm this, however. If he came to bed, he found me sound asleep and did not disturb me."

"I confess that I am at a loss as to where to go next," Huff said later as he and Beede sat in the taproom at the tavern late that evening. "I suppose we should interview all of Turner's neighbors, although I doubt that it will do much good."

"Somebody might have seen something, and we should grasp every opportunity to learn what happened," Beede said. "But I agree that we will not acquire much information in that manner. The houses in the west village, for the most part, are not visible to their neighbors. Unless someone was working in his fields at precisely the right place and at precisely the right time, it's unlikely that they would have witnessed the crime. And I don't doubt that a neighbor, having seen a murder, would feel it his duty to report it."

"So far, the neighbors don't seem aware of the crime," Huff said. "But it's a place to begin, at least, and I can think of no other."

Huff rose to order another round of drinks from the landlord. He returned with full tankards and set one of them before Beede. From the other, he took an enormous mouthful of rum toddy, swishing it around over his teeth and gums in what Beede took to be an effort to deaden pain. Like many people, Huff complained habitually of toothache.

"I continue to think," Beede said, "about Turner's mare. Was it released, do you suppose, or driven, or ridden away as you suggested?"

Huff nodded. "You're thinking that if we find the horse, we may also find the murderer? It's certainly possible."

"Failing that, locating the horse may at least point in the direction our searches should take us," Beede said.

"I'm sure you realize that if we initiate inquiries the entire township will know of Frank's murder," Huff said. "Do we want to do this?"

"No," said Beede. "But we have no choice that I can see, and the news will travel quickly enough, whether we will it or not. If people learn of this from us, we may at least be in a position to put a damper on some of the more outrageous rumors that will arise."

They did not find Turner's mare the next day. Nor did they find a shovel that might have served as the murder weapon. Starting in the vicinity of the

Turner farm, Beede and Huff visited every farmhouse and searched every barn in the village, without success. They extended their search still farther to the west but fared no better.

"I'm at a loss to know where to search farther," Huff said finally, after two days on the road. "We should extend our search farther still, I suppose, but I believe we'll face diminishing returns the farther we go."

"It would not be possible for the return to diminish further," Beede said, sharing Huff's frustration. "What could be less fruitful than nothing?"

"So what should we do next? And where shall we search?"

"We have already searched farther than the murderer would likely have traveled in a day," Beede said. "One would think we'd have unearthed some sort of clue to his whereabouts by now, and yet we have found no one to confirm seeing a man and a mare. Perhaps we should reorient our search and look closer to home."

"We've covered West Warrensboro pretty thoroughly. Where would you have us look now?"

"I've been thinking of our own village, Warrensboro Center," Beede said. "Perhaps the mare has been hidden right before our eyes."

Warrensboro Center, as the seat of town government, had been settled more densely than West Warrensboro, where the Turner farm lay, and their search, in consequence, required more time in order to effect a thorough investigation. They had no more success than they had experienced previously, however, until the end of the second day. On that day they found themselves knocking at the door of the squire himself, Deborah's father, old Israel Tomkins.

"No, I've not seen Turner's mare," Tomkins said with some asperity. "Don't you think I would have recognized it? She's been stabled here before, after all."

"I'm certain that that is true," said Beede, "but it would ease our minds if we were able to verify this with our own eyes."

Tomkins turned away, waving his hand in dismissal. "Go ahead," he said. "You'll find no horse in my barn, neither mare nor stallion nor gelding. I have only that chestnut mare that has been in my possession for five years, and she is put to the plow in my south fields."

They thanked Tomkins for granting permission to search the barn, but as he had said, there were no horses there. It became clear immediately upon entering that only one stall had been in use, presumably by Tomkins's own chestnut. They were both familiar with Tomkins's horse and would recognize it if they found it pulling a plow. It would be necessary to look for the horse in the field, of course, but it seemed likely that that horse, when they spied it, would prove to be Tomkins's own mare.

"I suppose we must go to the fields now," Beede said. He ambled slowly toward the door, discouragement slowing his steps. But Huff called out to him.

"Mr. Beede, wait a moment!"

Beede turned to see that Huff was studying an implement lying in the straw. It was a shovel.

"And is this dark brown stain what I think it is?" Huff asked.

Beede peered closely at the discoloration that spread out from the deepest point of the shovel blade.

"Yes, I believe so," he said with a sinking feeling. "I believe it is blood."

"It is not mine," said Tomkins. "I have a shovel, of course, but mine has a much shorter handle. Are you certain that this was found in my barn?"

"Quite certain," said Huff. "Do you have any idea why it might have been left on your property?"

"Why, to divert suspicion in my direction, I suppose. That seems clear," Tomkins said. "Although I've no idea why it might be done—or who might have done it."

"Perhaps the purpose was not to divert suspicion to you," Beede said, after a moment's thought. "The purpose may have been to divert suspicion to Deborah."

"A woman kills her husband?" Tomkins said. "How credible would such a scenario be? Remember they were married such a short time."

"It is not unknown," Huff said.

"Yes, of course, but surely no one would suspect a young woman so recently wed would be willing to murder the man to whom she had promised fealty."

"Marriage can unleash strange and terrible passions," Huff replied. It occurred to Beede that Huff would know this better than most; the domestic altercations that emanated from the Huff household were notorious. "And affection can turn to hatred in an instant."

"But Deborah is my daughter," Tomkins pointed out. "I know her fortitude. I know her character, and I assure you that she would not contemplate murder, no matter how distressing her situation. It is not in her nature."

"However," Huff said quietly to Beede as they left the Tomkins farm, "fathers cannot see through their daughters' eyes, or into their daughters' hearts. I am not so eager to rule out Deborah as a possible suspect."

"I find it difficult to imagine Deborah as a murderer," Beede replied.

"Perhaps you are correct in your objection, sir," said Huff. "Indeed, I wish it as much as you. But I would urge you to keep an open mind on the matter. She is certainly strong enough to wield a shovel, and she could kill if her victim were looking the other way."

"There is the question of motive," Beede said. "Why would she do such a thing?"

"I'm surprised at you, Mr. Beede," Huff said. "She might do so in order to correct an earlier mistake. If she had married the wrong man, for example, she might find it expedient to eliminate him in order to free herself for another. Surely this has also occurred to you."

"It had not."

"I see," Huff said. "Well, then, it is perhaps time that you consider it. I bid you good day, for now."

He ambled away from the Tomkins barn in the direction of the town green and his home, leaving Beede awash in a tide of confusion.

Chapter 11

Much against his will, Beede considered Huff's suggestion. Although he thought it unlikely that Deborah would have killed her husband knowing what he knew of her character, he found that he could not rule out Huff's suggestion entirely.

In saying Deborah might want to "free herself for another," Huff was clearly referring to Beede. Beede was too aware of his own shortcomings to believe that he would inspire such devotion in a woman. But did Deborah share this awareness of his weaknesses of character? Perhaps not; most of the people he met were only too willing to accept him as the hero that popular legend made him out to be. Indeed, Andrew Jackson, who had met him on the battlefield in New Orleans and knew him better than most, seemed to have bought the legend in its entirety. In fact, Jackson himself was instrumental in creating it. Deborah was much younger than Old Hickory—younger, indeed, than Beede himself—and might find the legends all too credible.

Beede sat heavily on a nearby tree stump and thought. In the absence of evidence to the contrary, he concluded ruefully, she might well have accepted the popular conception of his courage and integrity. In such a case, it was clear, he would be at least indirectly responsible for fostering her mistaken notions. His halfhearted objections to the popular wisdom would hardly be an adequate defense on the Day of Judgment. It was bad enough to be guilty of the sin of pride; to be the instrument of sin in others would be truly unforgivable.

Not for the first time, he reflected that a reputation for heroism could be as much curse as blessing. It required that he adhere to standards of behavior not obligatory for others and imposed on him greater sanctions than for the shortcomings of others.

There were greater responsibilities, also, for those so elevated by their peers. Those responsibilities elevated George Washington and Andrew Jackson to the presidency and burdened them with accountability for the fate of an entire nation. Both men had risen to the challenge; he wondered if General Harrison might also have achieved greatness.

Was it possible that Washington and Jackson—and Harrison, also—were less than heroic? Were they also the victims of public adulation run mad, forced into positions of eminence against their will?

He shook his head. Not Washington, from what he

had heard of the man, and not Jackson, based on his personal knowledge. And not Harrison, either, from all accounts. Harrison was, after all, the first man actually to have campaigned personally—even eagerly—for the presidency. These were not reluctant heroes; they were men of vision who saw their objectives and worked actively to achieve them.

That, he reflected, was the difference between true heroes and men like him, who drifted with the current like fallen leaves in autumn. And while he might occasionally wish to be a true hero, rather than a sham, he knew he was incapable of taking that necessary step.

Some might say he was doomed to a life based on falsehood. Nathaniel Gray, Beede's pastor, might call it predestination.

Beede caught himself, annoyed that he had let himself veer so close to the sin of self-pity. He forced his thoughts back to the work at hand. His present task was to discover the identity of the murderer of Frank Turner. To that end, he should track down Turner's mare and determine what had happened to her since the murder. He could also question Deborah regarding her possible motive for killing her husband.

He chose the lesser of the evils; he chose to search for the horse. His last stop in Warrensboro happened to be the parsonage, where Pastor Gray said—rather vehemently, Beede thought—that he had never seen Turner's mare and would not have recognized it if he had.

Beede thanked him for his time and prepared to leave when Gray called to him.

"Have you given further thought to my proposal?" the pastor asked. Beede was taken aback and had to think for a minute.

"What proposal is that?"

"Surely you haven't forgotten," Gray said. "I proposed that you should pay court to my daughter. She has been waiting eagerly, I dare say hopefully, for you to call upon her."

Mercy. Beede did remember at last. It had been nearly two years since Gray had made his initial request, and Beede had put it out of his mind. In fact, he had not taken the request seriously. Gray seemed to consider Beede a model of respectability, one who could save his daughter from falling prey to rogues and scoundrels. Beede knew he was not such a man and secretly detested being thought of in that way.

And Mercy was the sort of girl who would attract rogues. She was, inarguably, the prettiest girl in the town—indeed in several towns. She was cheerful and flirtatious and her fair hair and complexion and willowy form caught the eye of every man who saw her. For some men she would, Beede thought, be an irresistible enticement. Beede, who found her rather silly and shallow, was nonetheless flattered by her attentions and, though he hated to admit it, excited by her coquetry.

He realized why he had not paid court to the pastor's beautiful daughter; he had set his sights on Deborah Tomkins. In truth, he realized also, his sights were still set on Deborah, now the widow Turner.

•   •   •

Turner's horse, when finally found, was being cared for at a farm about ten miles away. It had been found wandering aimlessly in a pasture. The farmer whose pasture it was, had retrieved the animal, boarded it in his barn, and inquired among his neighbors. Eventually, word reached Warrensboro, and Beede rode over to take it in tow.

"She's a fine animal," the farmer said as he handed it over to Beede. "If you're ever of a mind to sell her, I might be interested in acquiring her. I put her to work on my plows, and she took to it like a duck to water."

"I'll pass word of your interest on to her owner," Beede said. "She doesn't belong to me."

"Not your horse? I wondered. She looks a bit like that mare that belongs to Frank Turner, over in West Warrensboro."

"You know her, then," Beede said. "How is that? West Warrensboro's some distance away."

"That's true," the farmer said. He aimed a wad of tobacco juice at the stone wall that served as a hog pen. "Frank's been known to come over this way now and again. I seen that mare of his tied up around town many times. Always admired it."

"Any idea why he'd come over this way? I wouldn't have thought this was a place he would visit often."

"Frank is quite sociable," the farmer said. "I don't doubt that he finds farm work boring and prefers to devote as little time to it as he can afford. He keeps his farm in good shape, but he is a social reformer at heart, who would do little else if he could have earned his living by doing good."

"Turner is dead," Beede said. "I'll pass your interest in the mare on to his widow. If she desires to sell the animal, I'm sure she'll be in touch with you."

Beede mounted his own horse and led the mare back to Warrensboro and the Tomkins farm, where Deborah seemed happy to see her. She listened to Beede's explanation of finding the animal in the nearby village and of the farmer's offer to buy her.

"I may very well consider his offer," she said. "But not just now. Everything has happened too quickly. I must have time to think about my future."

"Surely you won't return to Turner Farm," Beede said.

"I've not decided. It is a lonely place, but it is mine. After being my own mistress on my own farm, it would be difficult to return to being merely my mother's daughter—a permanent guest in my own home."

"I suppose that is true," Beede said.

"My larger concern, however, is expense. Can I survive on my own, even with hired help? I must think on it."

"We're pleased that you have come back to us," said Israel Tomkins that evening, as Beede and the Tomkins family conversed in the Tomkins sitting room. Supper had been completed hours earlier, as had the cleanup that followed.

"It's good to be back," Beede admitted. "I devoted

far too much time to the presidential campaign while longing to return to my home. I only wish I could stay longer, but I must return to Washington City."

"Must you?" said Deborah. "Surely you'll not be needed, now that the Whigs have gained the presidency."

"I'm afraid I must. I've been charged with an investigation that I do not feel I can turn down. According to Mr. Webster, it is precisely because I am a Jacksonian that I am well suited to the task. I've been asked to look into the circumstances of General Harrison's demise and to determine whether he might have been murdered. Mr. Webster seems to feel that a Democrat can be impartial in this undertaking in ways that a Whig could not. I'm not certain that I agree with him, but I was not able to persuade him of my views."

"Interesting," said Tomkins. "And who does he feel is a likely candidate for presidential assassin?"

"I've no idea," Beede said, "although I wonder whether he may suspect Mr. Tyler. He's been careful not to mention anyone specifically, but I have the sense that Mr. Tyler would be a leading candidate, even though Mr. Webster serves him as secretary of state."

Tomkins was thoughtful. "As a Whig myself, I find such speculation distasteful in the extreme," he said. "Nevertheless, I can see how 'the Godlike Daniel' might have come up with that idea. What do you think? Is he correct?"

"I don't know. That is why I must return to Washington City," Beede said. "To determine the truth."

"Did Mr. Webster have an idea of motive?" Deborah asked. "Did he suggest a reason why someone might want General Harrison killed? If so, I should think that might point toward his killer."

"If he was killed," Tomkins added. "And if the killer had a motive. It is not unknown for a man to be killed for no reason, or for no apparent reason."

"Such murders are rarely as carefully planned as this one would have been, if it was a murder," Beede said. "To poison a man slowly over a period of several weeks—that takes planning. If General Harrison was murdered, it was not a crime of passion. It could only have been the product of cold calculation. That is where I see a stumbling block. Who could possibly have resented the man to such an extent—a man who went to considerable lengths to avoid any sort of offense to anyone?"

"Who, indeed?" agreed Tomkins. "Except . . ."

"Except who?"

Tomkins shook his head as if dismissing the idea that had come to him so suddenly.

"I was just thinking . . . except, perhaps, an Indian."

Chapter 12

Although the trip back to Washington City was much quicker than it had been previously, a development due entirely to the railroad, it was no more comfortable. Beede was accustomed to the hardship of travel, but travel by rail brought new hazards that he would not have imagined previously. Stagecoach passengers often arrived at their destinations coated with dust from the road, which blew in almost constantly through the makeshift windows. Rail passengers were spared some of the dust, but they were bombarded by smoke and cinders from the locomotive. On long journeys, travelers would arrive smelling of wood smoke, their clothing blackened, often with marks from burning cinders disfiguring their clothing and their features, and their ears would be ringing from the constant, oppressive noise.

Most travelers put up with the inconveniences and the dangers for the sake of speed. At the breakneck pace of fifteen to twenty miles per hour, a trip by rail seemed breathtakingly fast after years of travel by stagecoach.

On his trip to New Hampshire, Beede had taken in the amazing speed, as well as the inconveniences, of railroad travel and had thought often about its ramifications. Returning to Washington City was different, engrossed as he was in the interesting possibility that Israel Tomkins had raised, almost as an afterthought, in his mind.

An Indian.

He wondered why the possibility had not occurred to him sooner. Who would have more reason to remove Harrison from this earth than an Indian, perhaps a member of Chief Tecumseh's Shawnee confederation, possibly even Tecumseh himself? He was widely believed to have died during the Indian wars, but some continued to express their doubts. There were several stories about the manner of his death, many of which conflicted with the others, and no one could point to the chief's final resting place. Perhaps he had not died in battle; perhaps he had remained alive, in hiding, awaiting the opportunity to avenge the defeat of his people.

It was a plausible theory, he thought. The fatal battle had occurred nearly thirty years ago, so Tecumseh would be an old man by now. But Harrison himself was an old man, and he had survived until recently. The man generally credited with killing the chief also

still lived. He had served—until a few months ago—
as Vice President of the United States.

Richard Mentor Johnson of Kentucky. Beede considered what he knew of the man; it wasn't much.

He would be, Beede guessed, in his sixties by now
but—by all accounts—still hale and hearty. He was
a Democrat, a staunch Jackson man. He had acquired
a reputation for heroism during the Indian wars,
which had certainly gone some distance toward establishing him in the public eye. He had also acquired
a considerable reputation for eccentricity in the years
since the wars. He had scandalized his native Kentucky by taking a slave as his common-law wife and
siring two daughters, whom he had worked tirelessly
to promote in society, against the wishes of the "better sort" of people. It was interesting, Beede thought,
that his "scandalous" behavior had not significantly
damaged his electability; Kentuckians continued to
elect him to state office.

And he had his supporters. Andrew Jackson, for
one, was a loyal and devoted friend, and Van Buren
had had nothing bad to say about him, either. Van
Buren, in fact, had used his considerable influence to
see to it that Johnson was selected as vice president.

Beede remembered Johnson as a coarse-grained
man with good instincts but without much in the way
of social graces and with a fondness for loud humor.
He was not easily intimidated by adversaries, as his
continuing campaigns to advance his daughters' position in society had demonstrated.

Where was he now? Did he return to Kentucky?
Had he chosen to remain in the capital?

A few hours of inquiry led Beede to conclude that Johnson had returned to Kentucky. For the time being, at least, he would have to look elsewhere for answers to his questions.

But there was work to be done. After making lodging arrangements in the city, he paid a call on Webster and found him at home.

"I had begun to think that you might never return," Webster said, in an accusatory tone, after greeting Beede at the door.

"I do not shirk my duty," Beede replied hotly. "However, my duty to you is only one of the responsibilities I carry."

Webster softened immediately. "Nevertheless, I'm happy to see you again," he said. "Are you prepared to pursue the matter we discussed previously?"

"I am. And with that in mind, what can you tell me about the death of Tecumseh?"

"The Shawnee war chief? Nothing much, I fear; I wasn't there, as I'm sure you know, and it occurred a very long time ago. Try Vice President Johnson. He's the man that killed him."

"I've heard his story."

"I see," Webster said. "Do you doubt him?"

"I've heard there are suspicions," Beede said. "No one actually seems to have witnessed the killing."

"That's a bit strange, I concede, considering how many people were there," Webster said.

"There were many people present, it's true, but most were preoccupied at the time."

Webster nodded. "Yes, I suppose killing other men and avoiding that fate for oneself would tend to distract one's attention. And I don't doubt that many men would be willing to take credit for that particular act."

"Many people did," Beede said. "But Vice President Johnson has ridden that horse further than most. I'm beginning to question—in my own mind—whether it's really his horse."

Webster had been pacing the floor. Now he sank into a rocker by the fire. "Does it matter?" he said after a moment. "As long as Tecumseh is truly and irrevocably dead, does it really matter who is personally responsible for the act? It's true that Johnson was all too eager to take the credit, but no one else seems to have a stronger claim. At least no one has come forward."

"I suppose I'm wondering whether the event actually took place at all," Beede said. "Was Tecumseh killed at the Battle of the Thames, or not?"

"I think you may set your mind at rest on that score," Webster said. "I myself saw a leather razor strap that was said to have been made from Tecumseh's skin. A rather gruesome souvenir, I would say, but effective nonetheless."

"But you were not there."

"I was a child at the time," Webster said. "As were you. And for that matter, even if he had survived the battle, Tecumseh would be an old man today. He would hardly be able to kill a man like Harrison."

"But not, perhaps, too old to inspire followers," Beede pointed out.

"Someone who took it on himself to avenge the death of his mentor? I suppose that would be possible, but I think it unlikely. How would an Indian get close enough to the general to murder him?"

"There you have me," Beede said. "He would be conspicuous, I'd think."

"Exactly. So even if Tecumseh somehow survived the battle and went into hiding for many years—which seems contrary to his nature—he would be easily recognizable by his dress and appearance. I do hope you will not confine your investigation to this unpromising line of inquiry."

"I shall not," Beede said. "On the other hand, neither shall I ignore it."

B eede allotted himself two days to determine what he could about the death of Tecumseh and the whereabouts of the chief's body. He interviewed a number of survivors of the Indian wars and could find no one who could say for certain that they had seen the man fall in battle.

"It weren't easy to tell one Indian from another, if truth be told," one old soldier told him. "They didn't wear uniforms, you know, and they didn't line up in formation, and they didn't have no regimental colors. And when it comes down to that, we didn't much care who was who. If they was Indian, we killed them. Simpler that way."

"So you can't say whether Tecumseh was killed in battle or not?"

"Well, I wouldn't say that," the soldier said. "There was several dead Indians there—one of them, I suspect, was Tecumseh."

"I am surprised, however," Beede said, "that no one took pains to determine whether Tecumseh was among the dead or the living. He was the most influential man in the Shawnee confederation. If you knew whether he was dead or alive, you would have been in a stronger position to defeat your adversaries."

"The Shawnee confederation pretty much fell apart after the battle," the soldier said. "That was good enough for me."

Having failed to establish whether the notorious Shawnee chief had been killed in battle, Beede reluctantly turned his attention to other suspects. The most likely suspect was President Tyler, who gained the office upon the death of General Harrison, but nothing he could learn about the man offered any reason for suspicion. After several days, he returned to Webster to admit his failure.

"In truth, I'm happy to hear it," Webster said. "I'd not like to think I was working for a murderer. I'd feel better if you could offer me some definitive proof, one way or the other, but I don't suppose that's possible."

"It's difficult to prove that a thing did not happen," Beede said. "I cannot say without question that General Harrison was not murdered, but neither can I point to any particular man and say that he is the culprit you seek."

"Regrettable, but understandable," Webster said. "I admit that I was beginning to believe that the old general had been done in—and that Mr. Tyler had done it. You have eased my mind considerably, and for that I thank you."

Beede stayed for dinner—"supper" they would have called it at home in New Hampshire—and talked into the night. Unlike the cold meal the two men had shared in the darkened house after the funeral of President Harrison, this meal was festive. The house was illuminated and the atmosphere celebratory. Beede at last met Webster's family, including his son Fletcher, who confirmed that he had been the one to bear the news of Harrison's death to Tyler at his home in Williamsburg.

"I went by train, by riverboat, and on horseback," Fletcher said. "Covered about two hundred miles, and that in a single day, more or less. I hope I never have to do that again."

"Rather impressive," Beede admitted.

"It's this new world we're living in," Fletcher said. "Ten, fifteen years ago I wouldn't have thought it possible. Now that I know it's possible, I'm still of two minds as to whether it's a good idea."

Chapter 13

The dreams had returned.

They had been intense in the beginning. When Louisa had arrived in New England, she would often awaken, screaming, in the dark, and Randolph would hold her until the trembling subsided. Eventually, sleep would come again, but it would be fitful. Often, she would awaken several times during the night.

The dreams followed a familiar pattern. She was running on a path through the bayous. A man—a white man—was following, and he was gaining on her. The events that followed would vary from night to night. Usually the dreams ended at a stream bank. She would attempt to enter the water, but she would be halted by a sense of dread that she could not define but neither could she defy. She would hear—feel, rather—the white man approaching from behind, and

the fear would overcome her. Once, in her dream, she
screwed up her courage and turned to face him, prepared to fight for her freedom, or die.

That dream was worst of all, for the man had no
face. And she would wake up screaming in sheer terror.

After several months, the dreams had subsided.
She was beginning to believe that the worst had
passed, that she was growing accustomed to her new
life as a free woman. She became engrossed in the
new, unfamiliar role of wife and mother, feeding,
dressing, and caring for a lively and affectionate
young girl. After a while she had almost forgotten the
dreams.

But now they were back, worse than before, if that
were possible. She suspected that the reappearance of
Josiah Beede in their lives was responsible for that.
She did not fear him, for he had always been kind to
her, but he brought back the memories of that fright-
ening time in New Orleans when her entire world
seemed about to collapse upon her head.

She sat upright in the bed, shivering in the dark despite the warm and sticky night air. She glanced over
at Randolph and was relieved to see that he was still
snoring softly beside her. He needed his sleep in order
to put in the long hours in the field that were required
in spring planting season.

Sleep would not return. The memory of her dream
had faded to mere wisps in her mind, but she knew
she would not be able to fall asleep again. Her heart
thundered in her chest, and the blood throbbed in her
head. She dared not make sudden movements for fear

that she might bring up everything she had eaten. Especially, she dared not lie down again.

She swung her legs over the side of the bed, walked carefully to the window, and raised the sash with as little noise as possible. She breathed deeply of the outside air and slowly exhaled.

It helped a bit. The nausea subsided.

She leaned her head out the window and breathed deeply once more, and as she did so she noticed—or thought she noticed—a flicker of movement on the ground, at the base of the house. It was only a moment, and then it was gone.

For a brief time she was uncertain as to what to do. Instinct told her to awaken Randolph, but he needed rest. So did she, of course, but she would not be pushing a plow behind a team of working steers in the morning. No, it would not be fair to disturb him.

The night was warm, and the three-quarter moon provided light by which to see. There was no reason why she should not investigate on her own.

She slipped quietly down the narrow staircase—as narrow as the servants' stairs in the southern homes she had worked in—and peered out through the slats in the closed shutters of the front room. She could see nothing; it would be necessary to open the door and step outside.

She hesitated at the front door but eventually opened it and peered timidly outside. She still saw nothing out of the ordinary; probably it had been a small animal of some sort fleeing for cover from a predatory owl or weasel. She was not a squirrel or a mouse; she was a grown woman and had nothing to fear from predators. For safety's sake, however, she picked up the broom from beside the door and raised it to shoulder height before stepping out into the night.

She felt childish as she crossed the threshold and thankful that no one was nearby to see her, a grown woman, wielding a broom for protection. What would her new neighbors say if they saw her like this? They would laugh, probably, and she would be forced to laugh with them.

She was, after all, no longer in the South. This was New England, where there were no slaves, and no one could harm her.

Chapter 14

Beede had been seeking Henry Clay at his house and in the halls of the Capitol building. When he finally caught up with Clay, however, it was on the street at the foot of Capitol Hill. Beede introduced himself and found that Clay had already been apprised of his assignment. While Webster was dark and solidly built, Clay was tall and fair, with a powerful though high-pitched voice. Beede, who had not seen Clay in action, could easily imagine the man holding the Senate spellbound with his reedy tenor, which would easily carry to the farthest row in the Senate chamber.

"I don't understand why Black Dan called on you for assistance," said the leader of the Whigs. "In truth, I don't understand what sort of assistance he has requested of you, nor do I understand why he needs assistance at all."

"Mr. Webster has asked me to study the circumstances of General Harrison's election, inauguration, and death," Beede said.

Clay wasn't buying it. "But you are a Jackson man, are you not?"

"I was. I am still, I suppose."

"And no doubt you voted for Mr. Van Buren."

"I did, and would again."

"Then I fail to see why we need you," Clay said again. "And unless you expect to find evidence of some sort of conspiracy, I don't see what you stand to gain, either. Are you hoping to prove that a Whig murdered our own standard bearer?"

"I have no preconceptions."

"Tyler!" Clay said suddenly. "Webster suspects Tyler! I should have seen it!"

"I don't know what—if anything—Mr. Webster suspects."

"It stands to reason," Clay said. "Who has the most to gain from Harrison's death? Why, the man who succeeds him in the President's House! It's perfect! I should have suspected him myself."

"I don't know that," Beede said.

"Find out, then! Losing a president is a tragic event, of course, but this would almost make it worthwhile."

"I have no reason to suspect Mr. Tyler's involvement," Beede said in protest.

"Well, I wouldn't put it past him," Clay said. "You know what he's being called? His Accidency. Old

John Quincy started calling him that, and it seemed so perfectly apt that others picked it up. But perhaps his ascendancy wasn't accidental, at all. Perhaps Tyler found a way to help it along a little. Oh, this is glorious!"

It occurred to Beede that Clay was remarkably cheerful about something that could be construed as disastrous for his political party.

"I have no evidence to suspect a conspiracy regarding General Harrison's death," he protested. "And if a conspiracy existed, I have no evidence to connect it to Mr. Tyler."

"Then find some!" Clay shouted. "It must be there. I've no doubt it will become apparent to you after a little investigation."

"I will investigate, as I have already promised Mr. Webster," Beede said. "But I will not create evidence where it does not exist."

"You won't have to," Clay assured him. "It's so logical, so obvious, that it should have been apparent to me from the beginning. The evidence you need must still exist. All you have to do is look."

"And if I do not find it?" Beede asked again.

"Then you must look harder," Clay said turning abruptly, making his manners, and continuing up the hill toward the Capitol.

The groundskeepers were still at work as Beede passed the President's House the following morning on his way to Webster's house across the park. Feeling no particular urgency, he stopped for a moment and watched the workmen, who seemed to be uprooting the same rose bushes they had been planting during his previous visit. As before, the young copper-colored man was supervising. He caught sight of Beede and approached him across the iron fence. He moved slowly, Beede noticed, as if he had been stricken by the gout, and the black scars had spread to his chest.

"Mr. Beede, is it not?" he said.

"And how are you, Mr. Panther?" Beede replied.

"Oh, tolerable, sir. Tolerable. No doubt you're curious as to what we're doing here. These roses are in a poor location; we're moving them to a spot where they'll receive more sun. I don't know why we didn't think of this before we planted them the first time."

"No doubt you had other things on your mind."

"Yes, that I did," said Panther, with a nod. "That I did. Well, good day to you, sir. It's been pleasant talking with you, but I must prod my employees a bit."

"Are they all employees?"

"You mean, are they employees rather than slaves? Yes sir, they are in my employ. I will have no slaves about me. Slaves can't be trusted, sir. Not at all." With a cheerful wave, the young man returned, limping, to his supervisory duties.

It had been a curious conversation, Beede thought, struck up for no apparent reason and leading to nothing in particular. Perhaps young Charles Panther—curious name, too—was starved for companionship, although he seemed personable enough. He supposed Panther felt he was forced by his profession to associate with people of lesser importance and welcomed the opportunity to converse with people of stature.

L ate that night in his lodgings, Beede again considered what he knew and what he suspected about Harrison's death. What he knew—he concluded grimly—was not much. William Henry Harrison had died in office. This had never happened before, and many people considered his death suspicious. Some were whispering about "usurpers" and "traitors" and were pointing the fingers of suspicion in several different directions.

It obviously pleased Clay to suspect John Tyler, the vice president who took office upon Harrison's death. Clay had hoped—indeed expected—to be president himself and took his failure to gain the Whig nomination with poor grace, refusing to accept an appointment to Harrison's administration

Beede had found nothing to raise suspicion toward Tyler. He was ambitious and wanted very much to be president, but that was hardly surprising. So did Clay, for that matter, and Webster himself, and probably a dozen others. There was John C. Calhoun, for example: a rabid states' rights Carolinian who switched party affiliations as some people changed for dinner, according to his current estimate of the benefits to his career. And Martin Van Buren persisted in the belief that his election defeat was an unfortunate accident that could—and would—be remedied at the next election.

Did he know that Tyler had murdered Harrison?

No, clearly not. Did he suspect it? He wasn't certain even of that. If Tyler had been at home in Williamsburg at the time, it would have been difficult to be the instrument of Harrison's death. It would have required an accomplice and to date there had been no indications of a conspiracy to murder the president. In fact there was no solid evidence that a murder had even occurred.

And if there had been a murder, was it possible that Indians had been involved? Again, no evidence, in either direction. It was widely thought that Tecumseh, the great Shawnee war chief of the previous generation, had been killed in battle, but no one with whom he had spoken was able to offer definitive proof or an eyewitness account of the event.

Perhaps, Beede thought, it would be necessary to pay another call upon the man generally credited with Tecumseh's death. Richard M. Johnson had ridden that reputation into the vice presidency, and he might be able to settle the matter once and for all. It would require a trip to Kentucky, and he was truly tired of traveling, but he could see no alternative.

Chapter 15

Louisa had seen no one the previous evening. She had searched the area near the front door without success. After several circuits of the house, she concluded that she had imagined the fleeting image she thought she had seen the night before. She returned to bed. Randolph had not awakened.

Now, in the morning sunlight, with Randolph away and working in the fields, she stared at the ground and saw what she had missed the night before: a path marked by trampled grass that led around the house toward a fallow field. She followed the path as far as the property line, where it disappeared in a woodlot belonging to Josiah Beede. She imagined briefly that Beede might have come calling the previous evening, before remembering that he was not here; he had returned to Washington City. The Beede house—and the farm—were occupied by five hired men, who worked (albeit reluctantly) under Randolph's supervision.

For a moment she allowed herself a sense of pride that the man she was beginning to think of as her husband had become a man who gave instruction and commands to others—even to white men. Randolph had taken to freedom with enthusiasm and an air of confidence that belied his past life as a slave. She wished that she had been blessed with that sense of certainty instead of continually imagining slave catchers lurking around every corner. Why could she not lessen her anxiety and enjoy her good fortune? She was a mother, she was free, and she was in New England, where slavery was illegal and her worries were behind her.

And yet, who had lurked around her house last night? And to what purpose?

Should she say something to Randolph? If she did, what could he do about it? She was under no illusion that there would be no consequences if he reacted in an aggressive manner. Randolph was a free man, but he was also a colored man, and it was naïve to believe he possessed the same rights as a white man, even here in New England.

In a quandary, she retraced her steps, searching for a clue—any clue—to the identity of the person who had lurked outside the house. This time she noticed that the grasses along this pathway had been trampled by someone with a long stride, which argued in favor of the lurker being a man. Other than determining that the lurker was human, and probably male, she learned nothing of value.

Still reluctant to take her concerns to Randolph, she searched her mind for an explanation.

Could the tracks have been made by someone taking a shortcut home? Perhaps. But where would this shortcut lead? Beede's house, certainly, was the most plausible destination.

One of the workmen staggering home from an evening spent at the tavern? It was certainly a possibility. An evening's tippling at the tavern might also explain why the path veered so close to Randolph's house. A drunkard might momentarily mistake this house for his true destination, and he might make a circuit of the house before concluding he was in the wrong place.

She felt the tension ease from her body as she considered this explanation. After all, she told herself, this was New England. There was little crime here. Most of her neighbors had no door locks, nor did she. If burglary had been the lurker's objective, it would have been no trouble simply to lift the string latch on the door and walk in.

And if an intruder were to enter the house, there would be little enough to steal. They were free, it was true, but they were also poor. They had nothing that a thief might want.

Except Louisa herself.

The thought stopped her in her tracks. Perhaps the trespasser had been a slave catcher, dispatched from New Orleans to take her back to New Orleans. She had been in New England only a short time, but she had already heard the tales of the slave catchers, working on contract for southern planters, capturing runaways and returning them to their owners. As the rumors had it, they were not averse to kidnapping free men of color and smuggling them into servitude, if they could count on a reward at the end of their quest.

Would anyone bother with her? Of course they would. America was a land of charlatans out for a quick dollar, and there could be no quicker dollar than an escaped slave.

There would be a reward offered for her, she knew. There would be a reward for Randolph, also. Even little Nancy would have value on the slave market if the slaver knew of her existence and wasn't scrupulous. Louisa had never heard of a scrupulous slaver. She doubted that such a thing existed.

Chapter 16

So, on to Kentucky.

Beede's route took him by stagecoach through the Cumberland Gap, then by riverboat down the Ohio River to the mouth of the Kentucky River and from there, after switching to a smaller riverboat, up the Kentucky River to Frankfort, the state capital. It was said that Colonel Johnson lived somewhere near there.

The trip was tiresome and surprisingly slow, considering that most of the distance was downstream. They were entering the height of the summer growing season, and low water typical of summertime plagued the sternwheeler riverboat nearly the entire way to Carrollton.

At some point—he was not certain when it had occurred—the land on the riverbank altered subtly.

From his position on the starboard rail, Beede saw the rugged mountains melt away to be replaced by rolling, grassy hills populated by horses and cattle, with only an occasional house.

The scene greatly resembled the Piedmont area of Virginia, not surprisingly. In fact, Kentucky had once been a part of Virginia, having been surveyed, mapped, and snapped up by several generations of exploration teams including the Great Man himself, George Washington. Now it was a state in its own right, though a sparsely populated one and, like the Old Dominion, a slave state.

It was ironic, Beede reflected, that the nation's foremost Kentuckian, Henry Clay, who sought compromise between slave states and free, often arguing the evils of slavery, was himself a slave holder.

No matter what might be your moral concerns, it was easy to see why slavery was economically feasible here—a meagerly populated land with good soil and a warm climate was convenient for big farms worked by cheap labor. And when it came to a conflict between morality and convenience, convenience almost always won.

At Carrollton, a smaller craft took him upstream on the Kentucky, and presently Frankfort came into view, nestled quietly in a crook of the river, seemingly dozing in the sunshine. It was smaller than Beede had expected, imagining that the capital city of a state as big in area as Kentucky would need also to be big. It sat on a low bluff overlooking the placid river.

Beede watched the deck crew tie the boat up to the

quay and then he started up the hill toward the town's main street. He did not know where Johnson lived, but experience told him that someone at the post office, or the nearest tavern, would be able to provide that information. Remembering Johnson from his days in Washington, Beede opted to start his search at a tavern.

His hunch paid off. "He's been in here today," said the innkeeper at the third tavern he visited. "He'll be in town somewhere, still, and you might as well start at the Capitol building. He spends considerable time there these days."

As it happened, Johnson found him about an hour later.

"Mr. Beede, isn't it? I'm told you've been looking for me."

Beede turned to see the man he was seeking walking behind him on the street. Beede had not seen Johnson for several years, but he knew he would never forget how he looked. The long face with its high forehead was topped by an unruly thatch of wiry gray hair. He would be in his sixties by now, Beede guessed, and most traces of the dashing young Indian fighter had dissipated. He was still tall, however, and he walked with the ramshackle gait that tall men often possessed.

"It's good to see you again, Colonel," Beede said. He offered his hand, which Johnson took in a two-handed grasp that was surprisingly firm. Although they had politics in common—they were both Democrats and Jackson men—Beede had never been especially close to Johnson. During Beede's years with

Jackson, Johnson had been a bulwark in the Senate, but Beede had moved away before Van Buren and Johnson took office on their own.

"I believe I heard that you were living in New Hampshire," Johnson said. "What brings you so far from home?"

"I came to see you on a matter of some importance," Beede said. "And it wasn't so very far. I was in Washington City on personal business, and I was enlisted in a matter of state. I believe you may be able to assist."

He explained the purpose of his mission, and Johnson snorted in response.

"Webster, you say? Are you consorting with the opposition now?"

"Only in this matter," Beede said. "And only because Mr. Webster is concerned about the import of recent events. In fact, he believes my Democratic ties may render me less partial in my investigation than if I were a Whig."

Johnson nodded in agreement. "I don't doubt that," he said. "Particularly since hardly anyone would have as much reason to kill General Harrison as Mr. Henry Clay. I don't say he did it, but I would not put it past him. But what is it that you think I can tell you? I left Washington City almost immediately after Harrison took office."

"I have some questions about Tecumseh," Beede said.

"Tecumseh has been dead for nigh onto thirty years," Johnson said.

"Are you certain?"

"Ah, so that's where you're going, is it? Well, come with me. I think this discussion calls for a tot or two of rum."

Johnson led Beede back into the town to a tavern with which he was obviously well acquainted. He refrained from speaking until they had placed their orders with the barkeep.

"Now," Johnson said. "Is Tecumseh truly dead? Is that not what you asked me? Do you doubt my honesty? My veracity?"

"I have no reason to doubt it."

"But you question whether I'm certain that Tecumseh is dead. Well, you're not the first to raise that issue, but you're the first in a long time. A very long time."

"I'm aware of your reputation as an Indian fighter, Colonel," Beede said. "I'm merely asking if you can be certain that you killed a particular Indian. This Indian."

Johnson regarded him for perhaps a minute before responding.

"To tell you the truth," he said, finally, "I'm not certain. I believe I did, but I can't say without question that I killed him. I believe Old Hickory said you were with him in New Orleans. Is that correct?"

"I was there, yes."

"Perhaps you'll remember how it was then. I was there, too. I killed a number of men on that day, but I couldn't tell you their names. I shot them—I'm certain of that—but I can't name them or describe them. Most times, I didn't even see them fall."

"The British were farther away at Chalmette than were the Indians at the Battle of the Thames," Beede said. "It would have been difficult to identify them."

"That's usually the way it is in battle," Johnson said. "I shot any number of men at the Thames, but I didn't introduce myself and shake their hands. And I killed one man who might have been Tecumseh. But I was wounded and losing blood, and they carried me off the field before I could determine that. One thing, though; he was a chief, an important warrior, anyways."

"Can you describe him for me?"

"Sort of," Johnson said. "Big fella. Not as big as me, you know, but powerful looking. Well muscled. A handsome buck, I expect the girls would have said."

"How old was he?"

"Couldn't tell. Might have been forty, forty-five. Old enough to be a chief, young enough and vigorous enough to be a war chief. The Shawnees, you know, have two chiefs—one for war and one for about everything else. Tecumseh was the war chief, and his brother—the one they called the Prophet—was the other one."

"You're sure you killed him?"

"Like I said, I was losing blood, so I didn't go feel his pulse or anything. But he sure looked dead from where I was. I didn't see him get up and walk away."

"Had you ever seen Tecumseh before this?"

He shook his head. "First and only time. That's why I'm not certain he's the one I killed. But people who did know him said that's who was lying on the ground there. Don't know why they'd lie to me about it."

Beede didn't either.

"Is it possible that someone else, a follower of Tecumseh who regrets how the war turned out, might seek revenge?" Beede asked.

Johnson was drinking corn whiskey, but he was not, apparently, a sipper. He lifted his shot glass now and tossed back the entire contents with a tip of his head. As he set down his glass the bartender arrived at his side and was already pouring another drink. Johnson took it, and the bartender simply shrugged and returned to his cage, leaving the bottle on the table.

"Possible?" Johnson said. "Yes. Likely? I think not. The Shawnee were pretty much demoralized after the Thames. They'd lost a passel of braves, lost control of much of their land, been slaughtered at Fort Meigs. Mostly, they slunk back to their villages with their tails between their legs."

"But later?" Beede asked. "Could memories of the defeat have festered until they felt they had to seek revenge?"

"Later? Of course. The question is: how much later? I expect most of them Indians are dead now. And for that matter, why kill Harrison? Why not me? I'm the man who killed the chief. At least I'm the one who gets the credit. You've heard the song they sing about me:

'Rumpsy dumpsy
'Rumpsy dumpsy

'Colonel Johnson
'Killed Tecumseh.' "

"Why Harrison and not Johnson? Interesting question," Beede said. "I don't know the answer just now. Maybe I'm looking for the answer in the wrong place. But it's the only lead I have at the moment."

"Not much of a lead, if you ask me," Johnson replied. "Mark my words, you'll do better looking at Clay for this. From what I hear, he thought the old general was going to roll over and play dead and let Clay run the country. I could have told him General Harrison was nobody's chess pawn, but Clay doesn't listen to Jackson men. I don't doubt that Clay was displeased to find that Harrison had ideas of his own about how the government might be run."

They stayed well into the evening. The rum and the corn whiskey kept flowing, and Johnson continued to talk. He seemed to have no pressing duties, and he was content to reminisce about the war. Beede was content to listen, for Johnson was, if nothing else, convivial. He had been, variously, a lawyer, a merchant, and a soldier, and he had served both in the state and national legislatures, despite laboring under a political liability of considerable proportions: his "unconventional living arrangements."

"Some of our greatest leaders have been attracted to slave women," he told Beede. "The difference between, say, Thomas Jefferson and me, is that I married mine. Those who object to this have problems of their own; God doesn't seem to have difficulties with it."

"And the electorate?" Beede asked. "Did voters have difficulty with it?"

"Some did. Some didn't," Johnson replied. "I have spent a considerable amount of time in public life—in the state legislature and in Congress, so I guess most folks weren't unduly exercised about it. And I was vice president, remember. So my 'defect'—if such it can be called—wasn't fatal."

"You were appointed by the Senate, however. You weren't elected Vice President."

"No one was elected Vice President that year. No candidate received sufficient votes, so the matter fell to the Senate to decide. I thank Mr. Van Buren for standing up for my election when even the Kentucky delegation refused to vote for me."

Johnson threw his head back, finished his drink, and slammed his glass on the table. He stood, unsteadily, and looked down at Beede.

"The important thing to remember," he said, "is that God was not offended by my actions. Only people. And not all people, at that."

He touched his hat to Beede and walked, swaying, to the door of the taproom. Beede watched as he turned to the left and made his uncertain way down the hall to the tavern's front door. Beede sought a room for the night.

Early the following day Beede boarded a riverboat for the return trip to Washington City. At

Wheeling, in Virginia, he stopped overnight, and in the morning, Beede inquired about stagecoach service to Washington City. Stagecoaches were notoriously uncomfortable—crowded, dusty, and more than a little dangerous—but they offered the only public conveyance to the capital.

The coach would leave shortly after noon. Beede had had little sleep on the boat, but he knew he would be even less likely to rest on the overland leg of his journey. Nevertheless, he purchased a through ticket and hastily gobbled a meal at the depot. Stagecoaches left punctually at the scheduled time, with little regard for the needs of passengers. Whether they would arrive at their destinations on time—or at all—was a matter left to fate. Most coachmen seemed to begrudge every minute of delay and drove as if the fiends of hell were hounding them, an approach that often created more calamity than not.

As he had feared, the coach was already crowded. Five more passengers boarded the coach with him, which virtually guaranteed that it would be an uncomfortable trip.

The coach started with a lurch, throwing Beede back against the seatback with a force that momentarily took his breath away. As he recovered his poise he took the opportunity to study his fellow passengers.

All the seats were occupied, as was usually the case with stagecoaches. There were six rows of seats. Seated across from him was a dark man who reminded Beede a bit of Daniel Webster. He was taller than Webster, however, and the lines in his face were

as deep as knife cuts. He had thinning hair swept back
from a widow's peak and his jaw was almost blue
from a layer of black stubble. Beside him was a dap-
per little man in a windowpane suit that would have
been more appropriate to the streets of Philadelphia
or Boston. He was accompanied by a boy of perhaps
ten years of age who was dressed in the threadbare
homespun of a farm boy and who watched the landscape pass outside the window as if he had never before seen trees.

The rest of the coach was filled with similar sorts
of people: a couple of traveling peddlers, a young
man—probably a farmer, also—accompanied by a
worn-down young woman who might have been his
wife. She held an infant tightly in her arms as if she
feared he might rise and run away. There were two Indians—Choctaw, by the look of them—and a couple
of professional men who might be lawyers, might be
ministers. The middle bench faced forward so Beede
could see only the backs of the heads of the passengers seated there.

They rode several miles before anyone spoke. It
was the dark man who spoke first.

"I know you, sir, I believe," he said to Beede.

"You do?"

"You're Beede. You're Andy Jackson's man. They
say you were in New Orleans for the big fracas down
there. Am I right?"

"I was there, yes."

"And you went to Washington with him, too, I
heard."

"That's correct," Beede said. The other occupants

were staring at him now with a mixture of curiosity and fury. He glanced at the two Indians, who had not reacted at all, as far as he could see. One of the professional men glared at him; Beede decided he must be a lawyer.

"You're a Yankee, ain't you?" the dark man said. "What're you doin' in Virginia?"

"I had business with Colonel Johnson in Kentucky."

"Johnson? The old vice president? So he went home after the election, did he? I figured he'd stay up there in Washington City where they put up with that sort of thing."

"I'm not sure I understand," Beede said.

"I'm talkin' about his livin' with a nigger, marryin' her and treatin' their kids just like white folks. That don't go over so well down here." The dark man spat tobacco juice in the general direction of the coach window. It missed the window and spattered the shins of one of the Indians, who did not visibly react.

"Sir," said the farmer. "You near hit my wife and baby with that wad. You need to improve your aim."

The dark man ignored him. "What kind of business?" he said to Beede.

"Pardon?"

"Pardon?" the man said, mockingly. "I said what kind of business did you have with Johnson?"

"Private business," said Beede. "Just between the two of us."

Beede waited for the man to continue his questioning, but he merely turned to the window and concentrated on the passing landscape.

"Colonel Johnson is a good man," said the younger of the two Indians. "He started a school for Choctaw. My boy went there."

"The best thing he done," the dark man said, "was to kill Indians. He was at Tippecanoe and Fallen Timbers. Hell, he killed ol' Tecumseh."

"He was good to Choctaw."

"Good to Choctaw," the dark man said, nodding smugly. "Good to Choctaw and good to niggers. Didn't do nothin' good for Americans, though."

"He saved me from the poorhouse," said the farmer. "He wrote the law that closed the debtors' prisons. You won't hear anything bad about him from me."

The dark man snorted and turned back to the window. They rode in silence to the next station, where the man left the coach.

At Frederick, Maryland, they changed horses and drivers. They had thirty minutes to wait before the coach was ready to leave again. Beede and his fellow travelers rushed to the tavern eating room and gobbled another silent meal, each passenger intent solely on acquiring as much nourishment as he or she could before they were forced to depart.

Another coach pulled in as Beede was returning to his seat, joining a new group of passengers he had not seen before. He gained a window seat and sat uncomfortably, watching as the second stagecoach discharged its passengers, who hurried into the tavern to endure the same tasteless meal he and his traveling companions had just experienced.

The new passengers were typical of his own trav-

eling companions except for one young man, darker
than most, who stood outside while the others rushed
to the tables inside. He turned briefly in Beede's direction, and Beede recognized the young man whom
he had last seen transplanting roses at the President's
House.

What was the name? Yes, Charles Panther. Beede
wondered if he was rushing to a new job farther west,
in Wheeling or Cincinnati. He called to Panther, who
recognized him and started in his direction, smiling
broadly. He moved even slower than he had when
Beede had last seen him, and Beede wondered fleet-
ingly if he was suffering from some illness more serious than the gout.

But he could only wonder. At that moment,
Beede's stagecoach again lurched forward, leaving
Panther standing in the dusty road.

Chapter 17

"These eggs are white," said Samuel Skinner. "I'll have trouble selling these. I've told you that before."

"And I tole you before that I don't have no hens that lay brown eggs," said Louisa. "These is all I got. Can't you do somethin' with them?"

Skinner shrugged and took the eggs from her. As proprietor of the village of Warrensboro's only store, he tried to maintain amicable relations with his neighbors.

"I'll do what I can, but I can't give you credit for them until they're gone. People 'round here have a thing about white eggshells. They like 'em brown."

"Well, give 'em back, then," Louisa said, reaching for the basket. "West Warrensboro ain't that far to walk. I'll just see how Mr. Jenkins over there feels about them. Maybe he got a customer what likes 'em like this."

"Wait a minute, Louisa," Skinner said. "Why do you have to be in such a rush? I'm just negotiating here, trying to get the best deal I can."

"I ain't got time to nego-shee-ate," Louisa said. "Little Nancy's growin' so fast I can't keep her in clothes. I got to get me some more cloth, and if you can't help me I gotta go on to the next village."

"Now hold on a little," Skinner said. "I don't want you to have to walk over to the next village if I can help you out here. I got some homespun just the other day that I can let you have, and we'll call it a fair trade for the eggs. Is that acceptable to you?"

"I guess so."

"Well you just wait a minute while I go get some of it. Calico all right?"

Skinner went into his storeroom, and Louisa permitted herself a small grin. White folks weren't so very smart after all, she thought.

When Randolph had first brought her to New England she had been frightened by all the white faces, but she was learning quickly. She did wish that there were more people of color around—people she could talk to and commiserate with. After Deborah, there was hardly anyone who could understand her situation, and Deborah was so young, and she was certainly white. Louisa tried not to be standoffish when she came into the village. She smiled at everyone and spoke to those who seemed willing to speak to her, but the white folks—most of them—would act as if she were invisible. Some would go out of their way to avoid recognizing her. She had thought, naïvely, that attitudes toward coloreds would be different in New England.

Skinner returned with a bolt of cloth and measured out the amount she specified. As he passed it over the counter to her, he said, "Did your friend see you the other day?"

"Who?"

"There was a man in here just a couple of days ago, asking about you and Randolph," Skinner said. "Said he was a friend of yours from Louisiana, asked for directions out to your farm."

"I don't have no friends in Louisiana," Louisa said. "Randolph don't either. All we got down there are owners and enemies."

"I don't know," Skinner said. "He was certainly friendly enough. He didn't act like he wished you harm."

"Bet he did, though," she said. "What's this fellow look like?"

"Well, he was a white man." Skinner launched immediately into a description of the man who had inquired after them. Louisa listened, and her heart rose up into her throat.

"Did he give a name?" she asked, dreading his answer.

"I believe he did, now that you mention it," Skinner replied. "I believe he said his name was 'Devall.' Does that sound familiar to you?"

•   •   •

There was still a crew working in the garden at the President's House, Beede noticed, but Charles Panther was not among them—hardly surprising since Beede had seen Panther only two days earlier, standing at the roadside, waiting, presumably, for a stagecoach heading in the opposite direction.

It was nothing to do with him, of course, but Beede wondered where, and why, Panther had gone, leaving his crew behind to finish the planting without him. He approached the fence and caught the eye of one of the workmen, the young blond man whose complexion had gone from bright pink to fiery red in the few days Beede had been gone.

"I see that Mr. Panther is not among you today," Beede said. "I hope he is well and not suffering from some illness."

The blond man leaned gingerly on his shovel.

"Charlie had to leave for a few days," he said. "He had some business to take care of back home—family business, I think."

"Family business? Does his family live nearby?"

"Not so you'd notice," the man said. "He don't actually have much family left, anymore, and what he has is out west somewhere. Kentucky or Tennessee. Maybe Ohio."

"His mother and father are deceased?"

"Well, his mother died last year. Charlie never knew his daddy. Never even knew his daddy's name, so I'm told. So now it's just Charlie and his sister. I think he was plannin' to stay with her while he did whatever he had to do."

"Is Panther also his sister's name?"

The man spat tobacco juice onto an aphid on a nearby rose bush.

"Panther ain't even Charlie's name," he said. "Not his real name, that he was born with. He just picked it up a couple years ago, almost out of the blue."

"Interesting," Beede said. "Any idea why?"

"No idea," the man said. "His mother's name was Jones. Maybe Charlie thought that was too plain for an up-and-coming businessman. It's the only thing I can figure."

"What did he have to do out west, do you think?"

"I don't rightly know," the blond man said. "Charlie never said, and I didn't ask. Seemed to me that was his own private business. You know Charlie, do you?"

"We've met."

"Well, he'll be back in a week or so. You can ask him yourself if it's any of your business."

The man sauntered away. Beede continued on his way to Webster's house, only to find that Webster was at the Capitol.

"I must say that I'm disappointed," Webster said when Beede found him at last in the corridors of the Capitol. They had retreated to a nearby tavern to discuss the possible next step in Beede's assignment and, indeed, whether there should be a next step.

"I understand," Beede replied. "I cannot say with certainty that Mr. Tyler was not the instigator of General Harrison's death, nor can I say that the general's death was accidental. It may well have occurred as reported—death by pneumonia. I have found no convincing evidence either way."

"Yes, I can see that," Webster said. "But you must have formed some tentative opinions on the matter. What do you think happened?"

Beede sighed.

"I've gone back and forth on this," he said. "At the moment, I'm inclined to think that Harrison died just as has been alleged: a victim of old age, disease, and his own foolishness."

Webster drained the rest of his rum and set the tankard down on the table with an air of finality.

"Are you comfortable with that conclusion?" he asked.

"At the moment, yes," Beede said. "Ask me tomorrow, and I may have an entirely different answer."

Webster gave this some thought. "If it became clear that General Harrison was murdered, who would you be inclined to suspect of the deed?"

"Senator Clay," Beede said.

"Henry? I confess I wouldn't have thought of him as a suspect. Why do you suspect him?"

"General Harrison was an obstacle to his control of the government," Beede said. "Senator Clay does not accept opposition with equanimity, I think."

Webster waved dismissively. "I forgot for a moment that you're a Jackson man," he said. "You're no doubt inclined to view attempts to strengthen the hand of the national government in the worst possible light. You probably oppose the national bank and the national road, as well."

"I'm of mixed mind about them," Beede said. "I

am *not* of two minds about Senator Clay. The man wanted to be President, and he acts like a man who resents opposition more than he fears defeat."

"Well, then," Webster said. "If you think he may have been involved, look into it further. Be discreet, mind you. I'd not have you casting aspersions on a man of Clay's stature without the evidence to back them up."

B eede remained, thinking, after Webster had returned to the Capitol. Webster seemed to doubt that Clay was culpable in Harrison's death. Beede wasn't sure he believed it, either, although Clay was the beneficiary, if anyone was.

But if not Clay, then who? Van Buren, who lost the election to Harrison, would not be devastated at Harrison's death, but killing his rival would not restore him to the presidency. For that, he would have to stand for the office again and overcome his opponent. Van Buren, in fact, had already begun talking about and making plans for the 1844 elections. That was his only route back to the President's House, and he would have gained nothing from Harrison's death.

Tyler benefited, of course, and he was clever enough to take advantage of the opportunity Harrison's death afforded him. He was quick to move when the opportunity arose. He had had himself sworn in immediately with the presidential oath of office, which established him in the office before Clay, or anyone else, could raise an objection.

Some might see this as unseemly ambition, but

Beede did not. A man *should* be ambitious, and the presidency was a worthy objective for one's ambitions to aspire to. But Tyler had not even been in the city during the two week period when Harrison had taken ill and died. It would be difficult in the extreme to murder a man from a distance of two hundred miles.

Once again the choice seemed to be reduced to Tecumseh, and Tecumseh was almost certainly dead. And even if Tecumseh, or one of his followers, had been involved, why would Harrison be the victim? Why not Richard Johnson, the man who probably killed the Shawnee chief?

None of it made sense, he concluded. He decided to put the matter aside and consider it again in the morning.

He fell asleep quickly and found himself, in his dream, once more on the battlefield at Chalmette, revisiting the events of that awful January day. It was the events of that day that had led to his brother's death in battle, that had brought him to Old Hickory's attention, and had set him on the path to national prominence.

But this dream did not follow the usual pattern. As he stared in horror out over the burned-out rice fields, he saw, once more, the ranks of scarlet-clad British regulars coming inexorably toward him and the little force of Americans. But suddenly—he was not certain when it had happened—the British were gone, replaced by hordes of Indians. It made sense in his dream, although he could not imagine why.

One Indian in particular stood out: a solid young

man who carried not a Kentucky long rifle like the
Americans or a musket like the British soldiers, but,
incongruously, a long-handled shovel. The man's face
was discolored by a number of dark lesions that had
begun to spread over his bare chest and muscular
arms.

Beede wondered what Charles Panther was doing
on the battlefield at Chalmette.

"**D**evall?" said Randolph. "Are you certain Skinner said 'Devall'?"

"That's what I heard," Louisa said. "You can go
ask him yourself if you want."

"I might just do that," Randolph said. "It makes no
sense. How would Devall find us? How would he
even know where to start looking for us?"

"Wouldn't be so hard," Louisa said. "He'd know
where Mr. Beede lived on account of the court
records in New Orleans. If I was lookin' for us, that's
where I'd start, too."

Randolph considered this and concluded that
Louisa was correct. It would not be difficult to determine their whereabouts if Devall were persistent
enough, and Devall was nothing if not persistent. He
had demonstrated his tenacity during Beede and Randolph's recent sojourn in New Orleans, when he had
attempted to acquire Randolph and Louisa as slaves.
Despite his own dubious standing, Devall had pur-
sued his objective with a civil court action that lingered for several months while Beede had labored
desperately to hold him off.

In the end, Devall had been unsuccessful, but he might well have decided to return to the effort again. On the face of it, it might seem that he would be assured of failure. But slavery, while illegal throughout New England, was not without its sympathizers even here. Franklin Pierce, New Hampshire's junior senator, had gone to school with southerners and had developed an appreciation for their customs and way of life. He was known to believe that slavery was inevitable and even, perhaps, a boon to mankind, and he seemed convinced that northern attempts to prevent the spread of slavery were unconstitutional. Pierce's beliefs were shared by, if not a majority, a significant number of New Hampshire citizens.

In Warrensboro, Randolph and Louisa had been accepted in the community, primarily by dint of their hard work and cooperative spirit, but Randolph remembered when it was not always so. When Louisa arrived, the community's opinion of Randolph seemed to improve, but it would take very little to set citizens against them once more.

It would be advisable, Randolph decided, to pursue this matter further. Devall might have no legal justification for following two people of color, but that fine point might be lost in the confusion if he acted on his intentions.

Randolph decided it was time to talk to Samuel Skinner personally.

Skinner's store was only three miles from Randolph's house, and Randolph walked it quickly, eager to learn whatever Skinner could tell him.

The store stood at one corner of the common in the

center village. It had been painted, but not recently, and was ready for another coat of paint. Randolph doubted that Skinner would do the job soon; like his neighbors, the storekeeper lived constantly on the edge of poverty—more than the neighbors, in fact, because his customers still preferred to barter rather than to buy.

Many old New England villages had common areas; newer villages rarely did. Even old villages were letting their village greens fall into disuse and suffer from neglect. They were originally intended to provide grazing for livestock—a communal pasture—but most farmers now had their own fields for that purpose. Warrensboro was no exception; today the common was used for storage—lumber to repair the meeting house had been stacked there for more than a year now. Randolph had grown accustomed to picking his way through the debris on his way to the store.

Skinner had seen him approach and met him at the door.

"I thought I'd see you today, after my talk with Louisa," said Skinner.

Randolph smiled briefly. Unlike many of his fellow townspeople, Skinner did not refuse to converse with a man of color, but he apparently drew the line at honorifics. In Skinner's mind, Randolph would never be a "Mister."

"You thought right," Randolph said. "Tell me about this man who calls himself Devall. Describe him for me."

"That's not hard," said Skinner. "Short and fat. He

had a wispy little moustache, rather dandified, I'd say.".

"Hair?"

"Dark. What he had of it."

The description would have fit the Devall Randolph remembered. A chill ran up his spine, suddenly.

"Where did this dandy come from? Where did he go when he left you?"

"He came from the south is all I know," Skinner said. "I don't know where he went when he left— presumably back the way he came."

"Was he alone?"

"As far as I could tell."

Randolph was tempted to strike out in a southerly direction, but he stopped himself. If Devall were truly nearby, he could only be seeking Louisa, or himself, or perhaps both. Louisa was alone in the house, except for Nancy. It would be irresponsible to go searching for Devall while his home was left unguarded. That would play directly into Devall's hands. Perhaps that was what Devall had been counting on when he let his presence be known. He must have known that storekeepers traffic as much in gossip as in goods and that the word of his arrival would eventually reach Randolph.

"Sound like someone you know?" Skinner asked.

"A bit," Randolph replied. "Hard to tell."

But Skinner noticed, when Randolph left the store, that he was visibly shaken.

Chapter 18

Devall!

The very name caused Randolph to shiver uncontrollably. It had had the same effect on Louisa.

A year ago, once they were safely onboard the riverboat from New Orleans, the tensions of their mission to Louisiana had begun to ease. After a few days, Randolph had allowed himself to believe that he and Louisa were safe. They were in the North, in a state that did not recognize slavery, and a sense of security had begun to settle in. Now he was being reminded that security, for people of color, could be illusory. Even in the North, colored men and women—and children—were not universally regarded as fellow humans, but rather as livestock on the hoof.

Randolph walked through the center village, conducting a cursory survey of every house and barn, attempting to deduce where Devall might be hiding. It was unlikely that he would conceal himself in a barn or stable. Devall did not strike Randolph as the kind of man who could make himself at home in a pile of hay or straw. But a quick survey of the village's two taverns turned up no sign of the man.

He knew he should go on to the west village, less than ten miles away, but he had left Louisa alone for two hours. If Devall were watching the house, he might have observed Randolph's departure and taken advantage of his absence. Randolph turned and headed back to the farm, and found, upon his arrival, that everything was as it had been. He was not as relieved by this as he felt he should be.

"No, I ain't seen him around," Louisa said, when he inquired about it. "And believe me, I been lookin'. He's the last person I want to see again, ever."

"I'd be happy to see him," Randolph said. "That way I'd know where he is. It's when I can't see him that I worry. What Skinner had to say was pretty convincing—Devall is around here somewhere, and we need to find him before he finds us."

"I figger he's found us already," Louisa said. She told him about hearing noises outside the house one night and catching a glimpse of something or someone scurrying away into the underbrush."

"You're sure it wasn't an animal of some sort?" Randolph asked. "A fox, or a wolf, even a hog?"

"Purty sure," she said. "The hogs I've knowed could move purty fast, but ain't none of 'em could do it on two legs, like this one done. Same for wolves.

Mind you I dint get as good a look as I wanted, but it was good enough. A hog walkin' upright I would of noticed."

"Then we must move quickly, before he carries out whatever plan he has in mind," Randolph said. "And I think we'll need help."

Randolph went, as he usually did when Beede was not around, to see old Israel Tomkins. He brought Louisa and Nancy along with him, for he was fearful of the consequences of leaving them behind. The four-mile walk was hard on a small child, but Randolph and Louisa spelled each other in carrying the girl on their shoulders. Nancy squealed with delight whenever Randolph took her up, which caused a thrill to course through him. He had not thought overmuch about fatherhood, either about its joys or its responsibilities, but he found that it gave him, on the whole, more pleasure than he could have imagined.

"Horsie!" Nancy said, with a shriek. She laughed. "Giddyup horsie!"

"I fear she has fallen in love with Mr. Beede's Morgan horse," Randolph said. "When we have acquired sufficient cash money, we may be forced to buy a horse, just to placate her."

"Ain't a horse a bit of a luxury?" Louisa said. "We ain't exactly rollin' in money."

"I know. But we could put it to use with the plowing and planting, too. It's an investment."

Louisa did not reply, for at that moment the center village appeared. The meeting house steeple poked up from over the crest of the hill. In a little while, they would see the common, and the Tomkins house at its far end.

"I, too, remember that man," Tomkins said. "I didn't care for him, either. But do you truly think he is here for some nefarious purpose?"

"I can't think of any reason for him to be here in New Hampshire, if not for that," Randolph said. "It was never clear to me what his business is, but I find it difficult to believe that his territory stretches as far as New England."

"But slavery is illegal here," Tomkins pointed out. "How could he hope to remove you from your home without being observed? You are known to us, and your disappearance would be noted."

"I don't know how," Randolph said. "That is what worries me most. Devall would not have come all this way without making preparations, so I must assume that he has a plan in mind—a plan that I'm not privy to."

"So what is your plan of action?"

Randolph shook his head. "I don't know that, either. All that I'm certain of is that I must have such a plan, and apparently I must develop it quickly. He is nearby, unquestionably, and I've no doubt he will strike swiftly and surely. I must be ready for him."

"You are welcome to stay here with us, if you like," Tomkins said. "There is safety in numbers, so they say."

"I cannot," Randolph said. "I have a farm to manage, and there is no one but me to do it. Perhaps Louisa and Nancy could stay with you for a while? I hate to ask it, considering our short acquaintance, but . . ."

"Nonsense," Tomkins said. "We have come to think of you as members of our own family. I confess I wouldn't have imagined, a few years ago, that I would ever say something like that. Nevertheless, it's true."

"Still, two extra mouths . . ."

"Will not be a problem. Deborah, for one, would not hear of it if I were to turn you away. She is fond of Louisa, and she dotes on Nancy."

So the matter was settled. Randolph knew he would miss his new family, but he told himself that it was not a permanent arrangement and would last only until the danger was averted. In the meantime, he could continue working his fields and, when not oc-cupied thusly, search for Devall.

The sun was sinking low in the sky as he said his farewells to Louisa and Nancy, paid his respects to Tomkins, and began the walk back to his farm, know-ing that, at least for a little while, Louisa and Nancy would be safe.

Chapter 19

Josiah Beede continued his inquiries about John Tyler, but his heart was not in it. He could find no one who might cast doubt on Tyler's whereabouts at the time Harrison had died. As a last resort he booked passage on a stagecoach to Richmond, and from there a riverboat to Williamsburg, where he thought he might find more useful information. Aside from a pleasant trip—the riverboat portion, at least—he came away with nothing. He suspected that he had found nothing because there was nothing to find.

Whatever suspicions Henry Clay harbored about him, John Tyler had done nothing to display the kind of naked ambition that Clay suspected. Beede had shared Clay's suspicion for a time, but it was a suspicion motivated by a lack other suspects. In the end, he was forced to conclude that Tyler was an unlikely murderer, having had a motive for the deed, perhaps, but not the opportunity.

On his return trip to Washington City, Beede mulled over the list of other possible suspects, as he had done many times before. As before, he returned inevitably to thoughts of Clay. Clay suspected Tyler of overweening ambition and arrogance, but these were terms that could be applied also to Clay himself, and with equal justice.

But Clay was also a well-known public figure—much better known than Tyler—and his movements would be much more public than Tyler's. Although Washington City was growing rapidly as the United States became more visible in the world, it remained still a small town, by world standards, and remarkably close. Everyone knew everyone, and secrets of such magnitude would be difficult to keep. He thought of his secret meeting with Webster, following the president's funeral, and he thought something of the sort would have been necessary if Clay were to order an assassination.

Beede had no doubt that the senator was capable of such a step, but it seemed foolhardy in the extreme. Even if he were to succeed, he would be replaced by Tyler, who would be even less likely to cede power to the Senate than was Harrison.

It was a circular pursuit, and it took him nowhere. He found it frustrating in the extreme.

There was, of course, one other possibility, which he hesitated to pursue: Tecumseh. The difficulty with Tecumseh as suspect, of course, was that he was dead—as definitive an argument as Beede could imagine. Beede kept an open mind about ghosts, but he could not imagine how a specter could murder a living creature.

It could be, he supposed, that a loyal follower of the Shawnee war chief might take it on himself to avenge the chief's death, but that conclusion raised even more questions. Could an Indian ever hope to get close enough to the president to cause his death, even indirectly? An Indian would be instantly recognized, and any attempt to approach the president would arouse suspicion.

Or perhaps not. A full-blood Indian might be instantly recognizable, but a mixed-breed Indian might be mistaken for a mulatto, or for some other variation. He remembered Jackson's stories of his frustration in fighting Seminoles along the Gulf coast. Escaped slaves had often been taken in and treated as if they were members of the tribe. The consequence, Jackson had said, was that his soldiers often did not know whether they were fighting Indians or Negroes.

It mattered little in the end because Jackson's troops killed both with little regard for whatever racial differences might exist. But elsewhere, it might be a different story. In New England, Negro men and women often paired up with Indians and raised multiracial families. As a rule, they were all treated by their neighbors as if they were Negroes.

An Indian who wanted to acquire some protective coloration might aspire to being considered a Negro. Indeed, as long as he was taken for a slave, there would be definite advantages to such a disguise; he would not be considered an equal to whites, but he might not be considered much of a threat, either.

So it was feasible. But did it happen? Was someone in the President's House an assassin?

Beede considered the men and women who had been close to Harrison. The President's House did not employ a large household staff, most of whom, like Martin Renahan, had been in this service for many years. It was small enough that Beede knew nearly all of them, and he could not picture any of them as a murderer. Furthermore, those domestic servants who were not paid by the government were the personal servants of the president; often presidents brought domestic servants with them from home. When the president was from the South, these personal servants were most likely slaves, but even presidents from the northern states tended to employ people of color as servants.

Ohio was not a slave state, but Virginia was, and Harrison was, at heart, a Virginian with deep roots in the slaveholding, tidewater South. It would be simple enough for him to commandeer a slave from the old homestead and put him to work in the President's House. And if that slave bore a grievance against Harrison, and longed for freedom, he might well resort to murder in order to cut the ties that bound him.

Afterward, of course, the assassin would do well to vanish. There were men and women in every part of the South—including Washington City—who would help him to escape. Most were slaves, but many were free people of color, whose hearts went out to those of their brethren still in bondage.

Had anyone in the household suddenly disappeared since Harrison's death? He made a note to himself to check the roster for runaways. If one were found, Beede had no desire to take up the pursuit. It would be enough to be able to tell Webster that a slave had mysteriously disappeared after the president's death and let the matter go at that. If Webster felt the need to pursue the runaway, it would be up to him to marshal the forces to do so. Beede wanted no part of that effort.

The Washington railroad depot sat in the shadow of the west front of the Capitol. From there, it was barely two miles from his lodging, so he elected to walk rather than hail a cab. This was not the most popular area of the city, populated as it was with low-rent boarding houses, brothels, and the city's largest slave market. As he passed it he wondered, idly, whether it resembled those markets he had visited in New Orleans when he and Randolph had been searching for Louisa. For a brief moment he considered entering it, for the sake of satisfying his curiosity, but he discarded the plan as unworthy.

Was slavery fated to be with us forever? Obviously, most of the people he knew in New Orleans believed that it would always exist. Kerrigan, the Manchester mill owner, believed so, also. Beede still clung to the hope that it would fail eventually of its own accord, but the existence of this bustling market less than a half mile from the United States Capitol seemed to belie that hope.

He passed the President's House on his way from the rail depot to his lodgings and realized that the gardening crew was much smaller than before. They seemed to be finishing their work and packing up their tools and implements. He recognized Charles Panther among the workmen. He was on the verge of passing on when Panther saw him and came hastening toward him.

"Mr. Beede! How good to see you again! I'm sorry I missed you last week."

"Yes, that was unfortunate."

"Had you been conducting business in Frederick?"

"It was just a way station, I'm afraid. I had been in Kentucky and was on my way back to Washington."

"Interesting. I, on the other hand, was on my way to Kentucky when we passed. Have you family in Kentucky?"

"No," Beede said. "I was there on a business matter. And you?"

"In my case, it was family," Panther said. "My mother died November last, and I've been trying to reconcile her affairs ever since. My sister still lives on the old farm, but as a woman, of course, there are matters that she cannot deal with effectively."

"Perhaps her husband . . ."

"Frankly, I'd rather he not get involved. I don't completely trust him, to tell you the truth. He's altogether too interested in my sister's probable inheritance for my liking."

"Is there much land involved?"

"No. Perhaps a couple hundred acres. But there are other considerations, which I'd rather not go into at the present moment. Let me simply say that I am suspicious of his intentions."

• • •

Beede passed the President's House again a week later and found that the workmen had gone. Remnants of the work crew were laboring at a house a few blocks away, but Panther was not with them.

"Mr. Panther has left you again, I see," he said to the blond man who seemed to be in charge in Panther's absence.

"That he has," the man replied. "More business back west. I'll be glad when it's all taken care of."

"He told me about it the other day," Beede said. "How his sister's husband has his eye on his late mother's property. It must be difficult to deal with problems such as that from a distance of so many miles."

"I'm sure it would be," the blond man said. "Of course, Charlie doesn't have any sister, so he don't need to worry about that."

"No sister? I'm certain he told me he had a sister."

"Then he was having you on," the man said. "Charlie's all by himself. Ain't nobody else."

"Why would he do that?"

The man shrugged. "Beats me. But Charlie's got his hand in all sorts of things he don't want others to know about. This could just be part of one of his schemes."

Josiah Beede sat alone that evening in a tavern near the President's Mansion, contemplating his situation. Frustration had been building for days, and it had reached a point of anguish that he had never experienced before.

He had always had confidence in his ability to see his way through problems. He knew a bit about human nature, he thought—about the needs and desires that motivated men to do the things they did, whether or not they were legal, or moral. He had always believed in his ability—almost a sixth sense—to decipher the motivations behind a man's actions.

But this was a new sort of problem. He could see all of the usual reasons why a man might commit a crime, but he could not decide whether a crime had, in fact, been committed. And such a simple crime, if a crime it was. Murder was so easy to accomplish. Without motive, it was almost impossible to point at an individual and say: "this man," or "that man."

He had not promised Webster that he would, or could, provide an indisputable conclusion, but he had not doubted that he could do so, until now. Now, it seemed, he might be forced to admit defeat. It angered him that an injustice might go without redress. More than that, it offended his sense of confidence in his own abilities.

He thought that, perhaps, it was time to face the truth; his reputation for solving crimes was as fallacious as his wartime reputation for heroism. He had spent weeks looking at the mystery surrounding the death of President Harrison and had, in the end, been unable to conclude even that a mystery existed.

It was time to go home, tail between his legs, and recede into the background where he belonged.

Chapter 20

Once again he chose the railroad: to Baltimore, to Philadelphia, to New York City, to Boston, and finally to Concord, where he redeemed his Morgan horse from the stable where it had been boarded, for the half-day ride home to Warrensboro. He realized he was becoming accustomed to the speed of travel that the railroad made possible. Would he be satisfied ever again with the slower pace and manifold discomforts of the stagecoach? Not that there were no discomforts associated with the railroad, but the speed at which they moved along made the discomforts far less noticeable.

After securing the release of his horse, he set out for the ten-mile ride to Warrensboro. He rode slowly, giving the horse its head, as he went through the process of mental readjustment to the pace of life in

New England. While he was there, he had not felt that life in Washington City was stressful or hectic, but now, as he rode unhurriedly home, the difference was made manifest. This was the pace of nature, not of man, and he had to teach himself to enjoy it again.

He stopped at his farm, on the near side of town, to observe the status of his holding, and was both pleased and vaguely bothered to find that it had been well husbanded during his absence. It told him that others could farm as well as he. Remembering the futility of his investigation into President Harrison's death, he rode on, finally, under a cloud of despair.

He stopped next at Randolph's farm and was surprised to find no one in the house. Puzzled, he tethered his horse and set out on foot to search for his friend. He found Randolph plowing a previously fallow field.

Randolph saw him approaching and waved.

"Home again," Randolph said, more a statement than a question.

"Yes," Beede replied. "And happy to be here, I think." He explained about his mission in Washington and its futile outcome.

"That doesn't sound like something about which to be discouraged," Randolph said. "It's quite possible, after all, that General Harrison did die of pneumonia as the doctors said. You cannot prove what did not happen."

"I wish I could be certain that it wasn't murder, however," Beede said.

"Some things may be beyond proof."

Beede looked around at the farm, which seemed—except for Randolph—almost deserted.

"What has happened here? When last I was home, you were a family man."

"That," said Randolph, "is a long story. If you've nothing pressing that must be done, please remain here with me while I finish this furrow. I'll tell you about it."

For the next three hours they worked side by side, trading off times behind the plow, picking out New Hampshire's ubiquitous rocks, and breaking up clots of earth. By the time the sun had begun to set, both men were ready to call it a day. Randolph then led the way back into town to have supper at the Tomkins farm.

"As a slave I helped out in the kitchen a bit, and I fancy myself as moderately skilled in its precincts," Randolph confided on the way. "However, I have a standing invitation with the Tomkins family, and I am usually too fatigued at the end of the day to begin the task of meal preparation, which is an all-day task in itself. Besides that, it permits me to see my wife and daughter, who are staying at the Tomkins farm."

"Why are they not here?" Beede asked.

"For safety's sake," Randolph said. He told Beede about Louisa seeing Devall—or someone she took to be Devall—lurking about the house late one night and about the man's appearance at Sam Skinner's store, inquiring about Randolph's whereabouts.

"I cannot watch over them every hour," Randolph said. "I dared not even leave the farm to purchase supplies for fear that Devall might appear while I was gone. Mr. Tomkins graciously offered to let them board at his farm, which has greatly relieved my mind."

"Are you certain that it was Devall she saw?" Beede asked. "If so, he is a long way from home."

"I haven't seen him myself, but I talked to Mr. Skinner. His description of the man was apt. I didn't think it wise to take chances."

"Probably not," Beede said. "You say you haven't seen the man yourself?"

"No. I searched throughout the village, describing him to my neighbors, but no one would admit to having seen him. I do not think that is conclusive, though. He could be boarding at a nearby village, where I might not have had the time to look."

"Then I will undertake the search myself, if you will permit me," Beede said. "Thanks to you, my farm appears to be in excellent condition, requiring little or no contribution from me, at present. I can afford to take some time to look for a two-legged rat."

"I would appreciate that," Randolph said. "When time allows I would be pleased to assist you."

Beede began his search in West Warrensboro. There was an East Warrensboro and a North Warrensboro, as well, but the western village was closest and nearly as densely populated as the center village. He went from door to door, inquiring about a small, plump man with dark hair and a wisp of a moustache. No one recalled seeing Devall.

He mounted the step to the last house in the village

and proceeded to knock before realizing that this was the Turner farmstead and that its mistress, the former Deborah Tomkins, was no longer in residence. Disappointed, he mounted his horse and proceeded to the east village.

At the third house in the east village, a man came to the door whom Beede recognized. He had brought legal action against the man in court on behalf of another resident some years ago, and the affair had ended unhappily for both sides. The man clearly recognized Beede.

"You're the last man I'd hoped to see today," the man, whose name was John Lovett, said. "Come to sue me again, are ye?"

"Nothing like that," Beede said. "I'm looking for someone. May I come in?"

Lovett shrugged and stood aside to permit him to enter, then stood in the center of the room—neither sitting nor offering a seat to Beede.

"I ain't been out of the house for a week," Lovett said. "My Bess is come down with something bad, and I have to stay and watch her all the time."

"I'm sorry. Warrensboro needs a doctor in the town."

"Don't want no doctor. If we had one I wouldn't call him. What with the bleeding and the dosing, doctors have killed more people than the smallpox. They won't get their hands on Bess, no matter how they beg."

Not an uncommon sentiment, Beede realized.

"Is there no one you can call on for help? As long

as I'm in the village, I can visit them and ask for assistance," he said.

"There's an old Indian up north of here that might be helpful if he's inclined to be," the man said. "He come by once before when Bess was having problems keeping her food down. He might could help."

"I'll find him," Beede said. "What's his name?"

"Don't know his name," the man said. "I just call him Squanto, like everybody else. If you go up to the north village and ask for Squanto, somebody'll lead you to him."

The "old Indian" called Squanto was, as it happened, no more than forty years of age, Beede guessed upon seeing him. He lived in a small, neat saltbox house on the fringe of the north village, with his Negro wife and two small children. He introduced himself to Beede as Jeremiah Lavender.

"Indians is so scarce around here that I've become an oddity," Lavender explained. "Since I'm the only one around, white folks figure they don't have to know my name. So I'm Squanto, if I like it or if I don't. It coulda been worse; they coulda called me Pocahontas."

"Are you Powhatan?"

"Wampanoag, I guess. My daddy wasn't part of no tribe, nuther. I figger I'm about three—four—generations from the wigwam. My kids is even farther, but they're still Indians to folks around here. Guess they always will be. Coulda been worse; they might have thought I was Negro, like my wife Clara."

"I see."

"I don't mind it so much, anymore," Lavender went on. "Used to upset me somethin' terrible when I was a youngster in school. There was two other Indians in school same time as me, and they wasn't too smart. I always got compared to them."

"What happened to them?"

"They died," Lavender said. "Smallpox, I think, but I was just a sprat and nobody ever told me for sure. Most Indians don't live a real long time up here. I been lucky so far."

Lavender agreed to accompany Beede back to the Lovett house. After saddling his horse and saying good-bye to his wife and children, he mounted up and rode off with Beede side by side.

"This is ol' Mrs. Lovett we're going to see?" he asked as they rode away.

"I imagine so."

"Don't know as I can do much for her. She ain't sick, I don't think. She just gets . . . depressed, I guess you'd say, and she sort of gives up on living. Not much I can do to help her with that."

"Then why do you go to see her?"

"Well, she seems to *think* I'm helpin' her. That sort of makes it worth the effort."

"I thought Indians had special healing powers," Beede said.

"Yeah, I heard that, too. Wish somebody'd tell me where I'm hiding those powers. They'd come in real handy."

Beede inquired about Devall, but Lavender shook his head.

"I ain't seen somebody like that, but that don't mean much. When I'm workin' in the field I don't pay a lot of attention to whoever passes by. Is this fellow an Indian?"

"I don't think so. I think he may be a light-skinned Negro."

"There's a lot of crossing over that line, I've noticed," Lavender said. "Indian to Negro, Negro to Indian. Depends on what people are expecting and whether you want to meet those expectations or not. If you find him, you might ask him."

"What will I learn from that?"

"Maybe nothing. Maybe a whole lot."

Chapter 21

Beede had begun to wonder if Louisa had been mistaken. Having systematically canvassed every dwelling he could think of in Warrensboro and having found no evidence of Devall, he found himself considering the possibility that Louisa had panicked at something—he could not imagine what it might have been—and had jumped to the unwarranted conclusion that the man had somehow followed her north to New Hampshire.

But it was Samuel Skinner—rather than Louisa— who had come up with the name "Devall" originally, and Skinner would have had no reason to mention it if the incident had not occurred. Beede had Randolph's assurance that Skinner had indeed said "Devall," an unusual name for this part of New England

and one unlikely to occur to someone who had not actually heard it.

But if Devall were here, where was he hiding?

Beede thought. He could, of course, spread his search farther afield, but he was rapidly approaching the point of diminishing returns. There were physical limits to the distance a man could travel, particularly if he intended to accomplish something at his destination that same day. A horse would extend the man's travel radius a bit, but the animal would have to be watered, fed, groomed, and otherwise maintained. That argued for a stable, or at least a barn.

Now, mounted on his own horse, Beede rode thoughtfully back toward Randolph's farm in Warrensboro Center, nearly unconscious of his surroundings. As he approached West Warrensboro, however, it occurred to him that he had not explored the Turner house. It was, presumably, Deborah's house now that her husband was dead without issue, but she had returned to her family in the center village.

Since she was not living in the house, Beede had assumed that it was now vacant. But perhaps it wasn't. For someone who was in hiding to avoid exposure, an empty dwelling would be ideal.

He rode to the Turner farm and quickly tied up in front. The house was silent and certainly appeared to be vacant, at first glance, but he took his time investigating.

A quick survey of the inside gave him no clues. It was laden with the dust of disuse, and he could see nothing to indicate that it had been occupied for some time. He climbed the narrow front stairs to a dormer room that had evidently been the Turners' bedchamber, but it was unoccupied, as he had expected. The bedclothes had been disturbed, however, and for a moment he felt a pang in his heart at the thought of Deborah lying there with her husband. He despised self-pity, but it took hold of him and gripped his heart and soul before he could shake it off.

He descended the stairs quickly and emerged in the front room, where he sat for a moment and thought, as he was wont to do when at his wit's end. For the first time, he took a moment to observe his surroundings.

It was not a comfortable room, and he thought Deborah would not have been happy here for very long. The only light came from a single window, placed up high in the front wall. It must be a very old house, he thought, built when the royal government would tax its colonists on the number of windows their houses possessed. It would be a dark house on a sunny day and nearly pitch black on a cloudy one. And cold, as well, all year long.

There would have to be a fire in the fireplace all day and all night, in summer as well as winter. This was the case in most houses, though, as the fireplace served not only for heating the rooms but for preparing the meals. The smell of wood smoke would permeate the walls and linger long after the house had been abandoned.

As it did now.

Beede had been rocking slowly while considering his surroundings. Now he stopped short and began to look more carefully around him. He realized suddenly that he was not smelling the residue of previous cook fires but new smoke from a recent fire.

He rose and strolled casually to the fireplace, where he picked up the poker hanging from a hook on the hearth. A brief exploration turned up not cold ash but feebly glowing coals, which spit at him as he prodded them.

This was not an abandoned fireplace, he realized, but rather its dormant but still-beating heart. The coals had not been extinguished; they had been merely banked for a while, to be prodded into life again in the not-too-distant future.

And, he thought, if the fire had not been abandoned, neither, probably, had the house. He began a second search, treading more carefully this time, seeking clues that he might have missed on the first search.

The search was inconclusive, notable more for what was missing than for what Beede could find.

Where, for instance, was the chamber pot in the bedroom? Every house had one, generally more than one, but there was none under the bed. It would have been taken out to be emptied, of course, but it would have been brought back, and quickly, so that it could be used again.

The absence of the chamber pot, so essential and yet so little noticed, worried him for no reason that he could identify. Without knowing exactly why, he felt certain that it had meaning, and that it was conveying a message to him, which he was so far unable to decipher.

Perhaps it was stolen? A chamber pot? Who would

steal such an item and why, except to use it in the manner for which it was intended? And this room—where people slept at night—would be the room in which such a pot would be most useful. There was a privy behind the house that would be adequate for the daylight hours; the pot was for those times when it would be inconvenient to make one's way to the privy, when one was dressed for bed.

He considered that the pot might have been broken and not yet replaced, but a quick look into the trash pit behind the house assured him that this was not the case. There were pottery shards in the pit, but nothing of the size and shape of a chamber pot.

There was one other place to look, although he could not think of any reason why the pot might have been taken there. The doors to the barn stood open since there was no longer any livestock on the farm and, therefore, no need to store forage.

He did not find the chamber pot, but he found evidence that the barn had been used—and used recently. Only one stall had been occupied, but the horse droppings were fresh, as was the straw strewn around on the earth floor.

Despite appearances, the Turner farmhouse was not vacant. It was in use, by someone who, apparently, preferred not to be noticed. Beede suspected that Devall, if Devall it was, had taken the chamber pot with him into hiding. If he found the pot, he would also find Devall, or at least his hiding place.

·   ·   ·

Beede returned to Randolph's farm and informed Randolph of his findings. Randolph agreed to accompany him back to the Turner house to assist in the search for Devall's hideout.

"I've heard that a station on the Underground Railroad exists—or existed—somewhere in Warrensboro," Randolph said. "Some opponents of slavery have a system for moving fugitive slaves north to Canada, escorting them by night and hiding them from pursuers during the day in secret compartments in their houses. Perhaps the Turner house is one of them."

"Deborah said nothing about it."

"She might not know about it. Such places, by their very nature, are well hidden. She was not married to Turner very long."

"It's difficult for me to imagine Turner as a friend to fugitive slaves," Beede said.

"I find it difficult to imagine, also," Randolph said. "Perhaps a relative, an ancestor built the space. It's conceivable, I suppose, that Turner, also, is unaware of its existence."

"Do you think that likely?" Beede asked, skeptically.

"No," Randolph admitted. "We may never know the answer to that, however."

The Turner house did not give up its secrets readily. They started at opposite ends—Beede in the cellar and Randolph upstairs—and searched carefully for signs of habitation. When they found none, they changed their approach to the problem; Beede went upstairs and Randolph to the cellar. They knocked on walls, listening carefully for hollow spaces. They found one, after a time, behind a bedroom wall, but a sustained inspection did not reveal the location of the entrance.

Beede and Randolph paid a visit to Deborah and her father. Neither could confirm the existence of a hideaway in the Turner house, although Tomkins had also heard rumors that Turner's grandfather had assisted runaway slaves.

"Frank certainly never mentioned it," said Deborah. "And he knew my feelings about slavery, though he didn't share them. If I had known it earlier, I might not have married him."

"Old Isaiah Turner was a Baptist," said Tomkins. "Very independent, like most Baptists. I would not be surprised to learn that he helped escort fugitive slaves to safety."

"Unlike his grandson," Beede said.

"Apparently so," said Tomkins. "Frank turned out quite different, in many ways, from his grandfather. I blame his education. He went to college at Bowdoin at about the same time as Senator Pierce, and you know how *he* has turned out. He might as well be a slaveholder himself."

"Not all Democrats support the 'peculiar institution,'" Beede pointed out.

"I'm aware of that, having met you," Tomkins said. "But I confess you're the first anti-slavery Democrat I've ever met. There can't be many of you around."

"More than you may think," Beede said. "And more will follow when the true nature of that institution becomes more apparent."

"I agree, especially as southerners attempt to expand their influence to the new territories to the west," Tomkins said. "It's hard enough for an honest farmer to compete as it is, without dealing with unpaid labor on those huge southern plantations."

Beede thought a moment. "I suppose there's a good chance that Devall is hiding away on Frank's farm. We should probably make a concerted effort to find his lair."

"I think that would be advisable," Tomkins said.

"Mr. Beede, may I have a word with you before you go?"

Beede turned and looked into the eyes of Deborah Tomkins Turner. She had followed them to the door as Beede and Randolph made their exit.

"Of course," he said, and waited expectantly. She shook her head.

"Privately," she said, and led the way outside. He stepped into the yard and found her waiting for him. Randolph took the hint and walked on ahead.

"I regret the necessity of bringing you even more bad news," Beede said. He felt it was his obligation to apologize immediately. Perhaps it would deter some of the anger he felt certain she would be feeling. To his surprise, she shrugged off his apology.

"I knew that Frank was involved in something of which I would not—indeed could not—approve," she said. "I did not know what it might be, and do not know still. But clearly it was something that I could not support, not that my support would have had any bearing on his actions. Most men care little for the opinions of a woman."

"What was it that caused your suspicions?"

"There were little things, at first," she said. "He would disappear from the farm for hours at a time, without explanation. Of course, he was not obligated to explain his actions to me, but a decent respect for others would, I thought, have compelled him to tell me something."

"When did this behavior begin?"

"Fairly recently," she said. "When we first wed, he seemed quite a different person or else I should not have agreed to the marriage. I believe marriage should entail companionship and mutual respect, and that requires a forthright exchange of views between husband and wife. I had believed, at first, that he shared this belief."

"His sudden secretiveness must then have concerned you," Beede said.

"Very much, all the more so because it seemed to be concerned with people who are dear to me."

"And they are . . ."

"Randolph and Louisa," she said. "And little Nancy, also. I do not, as I said, know what was involved, but I had begun to fear for their safety."

"And why was that?"

She shrugged her shoulders. "Call it woman's intuition, if you will. I cannot specify it further, but I had detected in Frank a degree of animosity, even contempt, toward them that I had not noticed earlier."

"Was this animosity of recent origin, do you think?"

"I do not know," she said. "It had become quite pronounced, however. Perhaps he had harbored these feelings for some time but had avoided expressing them earlier, until he felt our marriage was more secure. He knew how I felt about Randolph and Louisa."

"Interesting," Beede said. "Have you any idea of the nature of this hostility?"

"No, I do not," she said. "I think—although I am not certain—that it may have been their color."

"I believe Randolph said something to that effect a day or two ago," Beede said. "Mr. Turner, apparently, had attempted to persuade him to emigrate to Africa. Randolph said Mr. Turner seemed to take offense at his refusal."

"I knew nothing of that," she said. "Frank said not a word about it to me."

"Perhaps he suspected that you would be displeased."

"Perhaps he did," she said. "And indeed I would have been."

"No matter," Beede said. "Frank Turner is no longer with us, and our task now is to find his murderer and bring him to justice. I will say good-bye for the present, then, and return to my investigation."

He turned to go, but she called him back.

"I wanted to ask a question of you, sir," she reminded him.

"So you did say, and I inadvertently took our discussion in a different direction. Please accept my apologies."

"Apologies will not be necessary if you can answer my question," she said.

"I'll certainly do my best. What do you wish to know?"

"Thank you," she said. "What I wish to know is this: I once believed that I had won your trust and respect, perhaps even your affection in some measure."

"You are correct."

"Well, then, sir, my question is: What did I do—or fail to do—to lose them? Why have I fallen so far in your esteem? Please give me your answer, sir. I long to hear it."

"I beg your pardon?" Beede knew he was stalling for time, but Deborah's question had caught him off his guard.

Deborah sighed. "I merely asked how I could have fallen so low in your eyes. At one time I thought you felt some tenderness toward me, but now you seem to hold me in contempt."

"Not at all," Beede protested. "I hold great admiration for you. In fact . . ."

"Please, sir, do not patronize me. You have been back in Warrensboro for several weeks now, but you have not called upon me except to discuss matters of business. I had hoped that we might have been able to renew a social acquaintance by now, but it has not occurred."

"I have been reluctant to intrude upon your grief at the loss of your husband."

"Most admirable, I'm sure," she said, with a sprinkle of irony in her voice. "However, Frank has passed on, and I have not. I am not, as I'm certain you're aware, overly concerned with appearances. Further, my marriage was of extremely short duration. While Frank's demise was shocking and tragic, it was not devastating. I have come to an acceptance of it and would hope that you could do the same."

"I am trying to do so, Mrs. Turner," he said.

"You might begin," she said, "by calling me by my given name, Deborah. Friends need not stand on ceremony."

Chapter 22

"At last, we have him!" Randolph said that evening, as they sat before the fire discussing the day's developments.

"Alas, we do not," Beede said.

"Who else could it be?" Randolph replied. "Do you know of other people lurking in the area?"

"No, I do not," Beede said. "But neither do I know that the man hiding in the Turner house is Devall. Indeed, we don't know that the man who was hiding there is still there, or anywhere nearby."

"Do you not believe that we have found Devall?"

"On the contrary, I do believe that we know where he has been. But he is not there at this moment, and that is a major difficulty."

"Why do we not simply pick a place of concealment and wait for him to return?"

"Wait for how long? A day? A week? A month? And if he doesn't return, what then? And what if we find him? What shall we do then?"

"We could call Mr. Huff, the constable, to arrest him," Randolph said.

"On what grounds? For what offense? It is not illegal to visit New Hampshire, however we may wish that it were. Until we can discover him in an illegal act, or prove that one is planned, Mr. Huff has no authority to move against him."

"So we must wait until he captures Louisa and spirits her away?"

"We must wait until he shows his hand, at least," Beede said. "In the meantime, let us see what we can see."

Randolph frowned. "Let us hope," he said, "that he does not show his hand after it is too late."

They returned to the house that night and for several nights thereafter and hid in a nearby thicket to watch for Devall. Nothing out of the ordinary occurred. By the time another week had passed, even Randolph was beginning to doubt that Devall—if indeed it was he—would return. They began discussing other possibilities. Night after night without sleep was taking its toll, especially on Randolph, who was attempting to be a farmer by day while acting as a detective by night.

Beede watched his friend's growing difficulty remaining awake each day.

"Why don't you go home?" he finally said one

night. "You have a hard day's work ahead of you tomorrow. I can keep watch here."

"It is only sleep," Randolph said. "I can lose it. I cannot lose Louisa after what I went through to redeem her."

"You will be little help if you are asleep on your feet."

"I am all right."

They continued waiting and watching, but there was no movement at the house.

"I wonder," Randolph said finally, "if there could be another entrance." Without saying a word to Beede, he slipped away silently and returned perhaps a half hour later.

"As I thought, there's another entrance," he said in a whisper. "Devall could have been coming and going every night without our knowing it."

"Really?" Beede said. "Where is this entrance?"

"In the barn," Randolph said. "At the rear of the nearest stall is a false panel. I opened it and found a ladder leading downward. There must be a tunnel."

"You were not gone long enough to follow a tunnel."

"No, I was not," Randolph said. "Common sense got the better of me. I think this is a job for more than one man."

Randolph led the way. Unlike the interior of the house, the entrance to the passageway from the barn was crudely disguised. Beede realized he might have seen it before if he had thought to look for it during one of his trips to the barn.

"I think I should go first," Beede said as he began

climbing down the ladder. "Why don't you wait here and watch for Devall? There may be yet *another* entrance."

It was not a long wait before Beede reappeared and signaled to Randolph to follow.

"He is not here," Beede said, "but Devall—or someone—has been staying here recently." He led the way through the tunnel, which was unlit, by feeling his way along the wall.

"I believe there are fixtures for candles, or lanterns, along this wall," he said. "But we dare not let him know that we are coming. He is not in the hideout, but I suspect he may return at any moment."

They emerged from the tunnel into a narrow shaft, one wall of which was apparently the chimney. Randolph extended his hand and gingerly felt the stones.

"It's warm," he said. "It has been in use."

Another ladder led to an opening into a low-ceilinged windowless room little more than five feet square.

"This place would be dark even in daylight," Randolph said. "How can anyone see to find their way around?"

"I wondered about that myself," Beede said, "until I found this." He felt along the ceiling until he found a panel and pushed it up. The panel opened a small section of the roof, and moonlight flooded in.

"It's only a small section, but it makes the room a bit less dim," he said. "We can at least find our way around."

There was little to find, however. A pallet on the floor provided a hard bed. A tallow candle—cold now, of course—would provide some minimal light.

There was no extra clothing, or food, but there was a map. Beede spread it out. He could make out little detail in the dim moonlight, but he could see that it depicted the area around Warrensboro Center. One spot was circled, and Beede realized, with a start, that the circle encompassed his own house.

His house . . . and Randolph's.

Beede and Randolph discussed these developments later that evening and concluded, between them, that Devall had designs on Louisa, at least, and probably Randolph, as well. If he knew of the existence of Nancy, she would no doubt also become an object of his interest. Having failed to gain possession of Louisa previously in Louisiana, it had apparently become a matter of personal pride to Devall. Devall might be legally prevented from kidnapping slaves— or former slaves—in New Hampshire, but if he succeeded in doing so, the law would be moot. In fact, Beede noted, the law would have little or no power in the face of a *fait accompli*. It was, therefore, essential that they know Devall's plans in order to prevent them from coming to fruition.

They agreed to split the night watch between them. Randolph took the first watch, and Beede relieved him after midnight. It was a close-run thing, and Beede—to his chagrin and dismay—overslept the first night and arrived at the Turner farmhouse more than an hour later than he had intended. The upright clock in Randolph's front room sounded the hours softly.

He apologized to Randolph upon his arrival, but Randolph shrugged it off.

"He's in there," Randolph said. "I saw him slip into the barn when the moon was hardly above the horizon. He has not come out, I'm certain."

"Perhaps he has no duties tonight," Beede said. "But do not worry. I am wide awake after my extended nap, and he will not catch me unaware. Go home and rest." Randolph nodded shortly and slipped away.

It was boring, Beede thought, sitting in the thicket waiting for what he did not know but sensing that something momentous was brewing. To overcome the tendency to sleep (for he had not been entirely honest with his friend), he thought about what Devall might be planning. He felt certain that it involved Louisa and Randolph—and probably Nancy, if Devall knew of her existence—and that it also involved returning them to slavery.

How would he do this? By abduction, presumably. If Devall could do so, he would have Randolph and Louisa disappear from their world and reappear in his. This would not be a simple task. Randolph was well-known in Warrensboro by now, and Louisa was becoming so. The presence of their young daughter had made them much more visible to the townspeople than they might have been otherwise.

If they were to disappear, would anyone notice? Certainly they would, but perhaps not immediately. More important: would they care?

Some would. But would they raise the alarm?

Again, some would. But they might not notice for several days, which, for a man or woman of color, would be as good as a lifetime.

Was there movement at the house?

Beede stretched out on his belly in the stiff grass and stared intently at the barn door, where he thought he might have seen some movement.

It could not be Devall, unless Randolph had been mistaken previously about Devall's having already entered the house through the secret passageway earlier in the evening. The entrance to the secret hiding place was only through the barn, not through the house. Was it possible that Devall was receiving visitors? Was he, even now, plotting strategy?

That made sense, he decided. An abduction of a recognizable figure in the community, or two, or three, was likely to attract notice. Devall would need assistance and would most likely be forced to recruit his assistants locally. They would be pro-slavery, or at least not abolitionist, but it would not be difficult to find several such persons.

The figure was inside for nearly an hour. When it came out, it moved quickly in the direction of Warrensboro Center. Beede waited, to give the figure a lead, then fell in perhaps fifty yards behind. Once or twice, the man, Beede could tell it was a man now, would turn and glance over his shoulder, but Beede stayed in the shadows and believed that he had not been detected.

The day was coming on quickly, and Beede guessed they were only an hour or so before sunrise.

The moonless darkness slowly lightened into a form-less gray, making it more difficult for Beede to re-main unseen.

But if the early morning light made it more diffi-cult for Beede to remain unnoticed, it meant also that his quarry would be easier to follow. And as he watched the man walking ahead of him, he took on recognizable characteristics. His walk was familiar, although Beede could not yet put a name to him.

The man did not look behind him, so Beede was unable to see his face until they had reached the far end of the green. There, the man turned to look at the meeting house, and Beede was able to see him in pro-file. He recognized the man immediately, then, and the realization caused him to suck in his breath in shock and remain motionless so he would not be seen.

Nathaniel Gray. Pastor Gray.

Gray was not one of Beede's favorite persons, but he had not expected to learn that he was collaborating with slave catchers. Could there be some other expla-nation for his presence in the house?

What was Nathaniel Gray doing at the Turner house, which was supposedly vacant? He was not vis-iting Deborah, who had returned to her parents' home. He had known about the secret passageway from the barn, which surely was not common knowledge. Clearly, he knew someone was hiding there, and it could only be surmised that he knew *who* was hiding there.

Was it possible that Beede was leaping to conclu-sions? Perhaps Gray had visited the Turner house for some reason other than to provide aid and comfort to a slave catcher.

But if Gray had visited the Turner house for some legitimate purpose, he would not have waited until midnight to do so, and he would have entered through the door—not the secret passageway. And since the house was, nominally, vacant, what legitimate purpose for visiting could there be?

He could think of none.

Beede was forced to grasp the obvious conclusion: that Gray, Warrensboro's moral and spiritual leader, was secretly a supporter of slavery and a confidant of slavers.

It was not unheard of, he knew. Even in New England, where slavery was no longer legal, pro-slavery sentiment persisted in some quarters. Only a few years earlier, a mob in Massachusetts had attacked William Lloyd Garrison, the prominent abolitionist, and had almost succeeded in killing him in protest over his writings. Ministers of the Gospel were not exempt from such sentiment; some even justified their feelings with carefully chosen scriptural passages.

It seemed that Gray had successfully hidden his opinions from his congregation, however. Israel Tomkins, whom everyone called the squire of Warrensboro, would not have countenanced a pro-slavery minister in his church and would have led the opposition if he had known. Gray was apparently aware of this and had shrewdly kept his opinions to himself.

But it occurred to Beede that Gray would be well situated to recruit allies for Devall. As a permanent resident he would be in a position to know others who shared his views, and as a respected professional he would be able to rally their support when necessary.

Perhaps, Beede thought, it was time to consider joining another church, where the pastor was more in concordance with his own views. He wished mightily to do so. For the time being, however, he thought it might prove more profitable to remain in Gray's church—and to listen closely.

Chapter 23

He did so the following Sunday, but Gray made no mention of Devall, or slavery, or anything that might be construed as an admission by those who were aware of his opinion. The sermon was, nevertheless, instructive.

Randolph did not attend, as was his wont; he had been received coldly by the congregants on the few days he had attempted to worship there. In the South, many churches welcomed worshippers of both races, and Negro parishioners sometimes outnumbered whites. This was not the case in the North, as Randolph had discovered, and there were no Negro congregations within a radius of several miles.

It was as well, for Gray's sermons were trivial and tedious more often than not. Beede usually found his mind wandering to more secular concerns, no matter

how relentlessly he attempted to concentrate on what
he took to be the message of the day. Frequently, in
fact, he had considerable difficulty determining what
the message was.

On this particular Sunday, the message seemed to
be that man was depraved by nature and that those
who believed otherwise were dangerous. Beede believed the first part of the message but had doubts
about the second; Unitarians, in his experience, believed in the perfectability of mankind but were
largely harmless and ineffectual, hardly worth the
furor that orthodox Protestants had raised over their
curious theologies.

He was prepared to ignore the rest of Gray's sermon and turn his attention toward the problem of Devall, but the pastor caught his attention again with his
next remarks:

"Satan is abroad among mortal man!" Gray said.
"He would have us believe that he does not exist, but
he does exist. He lives with us every day, shares our
food and drink, and even sits among us in the meeting house on the Sabbath.

"We say we do not see him, have never seen him,
but we tell ourselves lies. He comes to us and whis-
pers in our ears. He tells us that we must live in this
world and abide by the laws of the world, and break
bread with those who would lead us into temptation."

Strange words, Beede thought, from a man of God.
Jesus went to sinners—tax collectors and Phar-
isees—and broke bread with them. Would Gray have
us wall ourselves off from others, to avoid the taint of
evil?

The pastor stopped to catch a breath but soon resumed.

"Man's days on earth are numbered, and his life is as nothing compared to the power and glory of God, who made us and set our feet on the paths of righteousness. It is His will that we wake in the morning to another day. Our gratitude must know no bounds, for His mercy is likewise boundless.

"And what does He ask of us in return? He asks that we continue to walk in righteousness, eschew sin, and spurn the temptations of the flesh.

"Others may flourish in the cesspools of the earth, but we—who love God and abhor iniquity—must stand like sentries against the gates of hell. The hordes of devils and demons are nearby, threatening to destroy the kingdom of God. We must be prepared to defend against them."

This, thought Beede, sounds like no sermon I have heard before, at least from Nathaniel Gray. Gray's sermons tended toward inoffensiveness. Beede had never before encountered the minister in an angry—not to mention vengeful—tone, but something clearly had ignited a spark of passion that must have been suspended somewhere in the back of his mind, and which he had at last permitted to come forth.

"But how will we know these—demons?" Gray continued. "In their superficial appearance, they resemble our friends and neighbors, for Satan has made them so. The differences between men and demons are often subtle, and we must take care to discern them."

Beede suddenly sensed that the sermon was mov-

ing in directions he had hoped it would avoid. Gray's
next sentence brought the realization to him transpar-
ently.

"The Bible tells us that God made man in His own
image. But what does that mean? That he walks on
two legs? Surely there must be more resemblance
than that. Gorillas can do that, but they cannot have
been made in the image of the Creator. Nor could it
be said of apes, or chickens, which also walk upright.
Nor Negroes or Chinamen, even though they may be
able to speak almost as we do."

Beede was astonished. He had never heard Gray
speak like this before. Were these his true sentiments?
It would explain why Randolph had never felt comfortable in this church.

The pastor continued to expound on the subject,
tying Negroes (to whom he referred only by allusion
at this point) to various Biblical events—the flood,
the plagues of Egypt, the destruction of Sodom and
Gomorrah—all of which seemed calculated to show
darker people in the worst possible light. He pro-
fessed to find connections that Beede had never imagined.

"The demons walk and talk and live among us,"
Gray then said. "We must be ever vigilant for our
souls' sake if we are not to fall victim to the temptations of the flesh."

It came to Beede suddenly that Gray's sermon had
become a thinly veiled diatribe against Randolph and
Louisa, the only people of color in the town. He was
seized by a rage that overcame his reason.

Hardly thinking of his actions, he stood suddenly

and eased his way out of the pew. In the aisle he turned and walked purposefully out of the meeting house. No one stopped him. Some turned to watch as he left.

Gray continued his sermon as if nothing untoward had happened.

Standing outside the church on the wooden banquette, Beede found that he was shaking in anger. He grabbed one of the Greek-style support columns and held on to it as tightly as he could until the shaking subsided. It required several minutes. He worried that someone might join him on the banquette to question his actions, but no one did. Eventually he decided he was calm enough to begin his journey home.

His plan to watch and listen had fallen apart at his own hands. He had intended to observe Gray's actions and extract some understanding of what the pastor might be about; now, by making a public show and walking out of the church, he had lost the opportunity.

Several days later, a knock was heard at the door of Randolph's house, where Beede had been staying. Randolph came to tell him that a visitor had arrived for him. He recognized the visitor immediately, with astonishment: Louisa Gray, the wife of the pastor, Nathaniel Gray.

"I hope I am not intruding, sir," she said.

"Not at all, Mrs. Gray. Please come in." It was Randolph's house, not his own, and by rights the invitation should have been extended by Randolph, but Beede forgot that, in his surprise.

"I shall inspect the cornfields," Randolph said.

"No, please," Beede said. "Stay with us. I daresay we have nothing to discuss that you cannot also hear." He could see that Mrs. Gray had other ideas, but he was not inclined to give them countenance.

Mrs. Gray evidently felt some reluctance about the situation, but she said nothing about it. She sat nervously in the room's only chair, while Beede and Randolph shared the bench by the fireplace.

"How may I help you, Mrs. Gray?" Beede said, finally, when she seemed loath to begin.

"Oh, sir, I find it difficult to explain the concerns of my heart, and yet I must do so for the sake of my family," she blurted. "I am at my wit's end."

"I'm sorry to hear it," Beede said. "Is there something I can do to relieve your mind?"

"I do not know," she said. "But you are the only person to whom I can turn. Someone must talk to my husband and redirect his steps."

Beede had been to the Grays' home on a few occasions, as had most of the pastor's congregation, but he had never considered himself to be a confidant of the minister or his household. He felt quite certain that the pastor did not consider him a close friend.

"I do not understand, Mrs. Gray," he said. "In what way should I attempt to, as you put it, redirect his steps. And couldn't you be much more successful at it than I? You are his wife, and you must be aware of his intimate thoughts."

"I am," she replied. "And that is the problem, sir. He is afflicted with the one sickness against which I am powerless."

"And that is . . .?"

"Lust, sir! My husband is enamored of another woman!"

"I regret to hear it," Beede said, still confused. "Do I know the woman?"

"Ah, yes sir—but Mr. Randolph knows her better. Mr. Gray is enamored of the other Louisa. Mr. Randolph's wife!"

"Louisa?" Randolph said, in amazement. "My Louisa?"

"Yes, sir. Surely this does not surprise you. She is a beautiful young woman. I'm certain this is not the first time that an otherwise prudent gentleman has been distracted by her wiles."

"I was unaware that Mr. Gray had even seen Louisa," Randolph said. "We do not frequently attend Sabbath services."

"But you live among us," Mrs. Gray said. "We are such a small community that it is impossible not to meet each other. I do not know how my husband became acquainted with your Louisa; perhaps he met her at Mr. Skinner's store, but you may be assured that he knows very well who she is."

"Why do you believe he is infatuated with the other Louisa?" Beede asked.

"A woman knows," Louisa Gray replied. "I knew almost immediately. He came home one day from . . . wherever he had been . . . and told me about meeting a brazen woman who shared my name. He called her a slut, actually. Since that time he has found cause to speak of her frequently every day. Almost anything can serve to remind him of her."

"He called my Louisa a slut?" Randolph said.

"I doubt that he meant to imply that she was promiscuous," Beede began.

"Certainly, he did," Louisa Gray overrode Beede's protestations. "The Negro people are known for their love of pleasure and their moral laxity. My husband is a deeply moral man, but there are temptations that no man can withstand. My Nathaniel is a man of God, but he is also human and vulnerable, like any other man."

"Are you implying that Louisa—Randolph's Louisa—has tempted Pastor Gray to sin?" Beede asked, incredulously.

"Certainly. My husband detests carnal behavior as much as any man of God, but he cannot endure temptation forever. If he were to succumb to her wiles, his life would be ruined, as would ours!"

Chapter 24

"**S**uccumb to my what? My *wiles*?" Louisa said, incredulously, when Randolph later recounted the matter to her. "And tell me again, who I'se supposed to be workin' my *wiles* on."

"Nathaniel Gray, the minister at the center church," said Randolph. "And wiles isn't my word; it's the word his wife used. I'm just passing along what she told us."

"Well, I remember *her* all right, but I ain't never met the man," Louisa said. "And him a preacher, you say? Where'd I supposed to have met him? Don't know no preachers, far as I know. Went to church here once or twice but didn't meet no preachers."

"He is a thin, gray-haired man with a long face," Beede said. "Rather cadaverous in appearance." He and Randolph had walked into the village to the

Tomkins house because Louisa and Nancy were still lodging with Israel Tomkins and his family. They stood in a patch of grass behind the house where they would not disturb—or be overheard by—Israel and his family.

"White men all look purty much alike to me," Louisa said after considering Beede's description of the pastor. "And that description don't help much. But it don't matter anyhow. If I met him I don't remember it. And if I don't remember, how could I be workin' my wiles on him?"

"I guess he's seen you, though," said Randolph.

"Can't help that. I live here now. I gotta walk around, go to the store, feed the chickens, look after Nancy. I can't quit livin' just to make life easier for some horny ol' preacher."

"No," said Beede. "You can't."

"So what should I do?" Louisa asked.

"Nothing you can do," said Beede. "Just watch out for strangers. If something untoward happens, we need to be able to move in and help you."

"I got my eyes open," Louisa said. "I ain't under any illusions. I lived in the South for a long time."

"You're not in the South anymore," Beede pointed out.

"Some things ain't changed, though," she replied. "If I'd a forgot that, you just reminded me."

Chapter 25

Back to Washington City. Beede was growing weary of the journey, but he could see no way to avoid it. There were issues still to be resolved regarding the president's death, and they could only be resolved there. Once more, he took the railroad, and once more he arrived at his destination wearing a filmy coating of ash and soot. The first time it had been an adventure to make the trip, but this was his third trip in as many months, and it was growing tiresome.

On arrival, he decided not to attempt to secure accommodations, hoping that his duties might not require a long stay. If he could find Panther quickly and obtain the answers he sought, he might be able to catch an early morning train back to New England. If so, he could pass the evening at the station, or in a nearby tavern, and save not only the money, but the time involved in taking a room for the night.

It took some time. The crew's work at the President's Mansion had been completed, apparently, for there were no signs of activity in the gardens there. Beede was forced to inquire throughout the city, at taverns, government offices, and mercantile establishments, until he learned that Panther's crews were working at a private residence near the city's western edge.

He spied Panther immediately at the new work site. Working shirtless, as was his habit, he looked to be in good form, but he moved with no alacrity, as if plagued by an overwhelming fatigue. Beede stood quietly at the wrought-iron fence of the residence, watching intently, until Panther noticed his presence.

"Mr. Beede. How are you today, sir?" said Panther. "I confess that I had not expected to see you again."

"I'm a bit surprised, myself," Beede admitted. "It was necessary for me to return to Washington City, however, to ask some questions of you."

"Of me, sir?" At that, Panther broke into a fit of coughing that lasted for some time. Beede waited patiently for the coughing spasms to recede before proceeding.

"Quite so," he said when the man's coughing had ceased. "I believe you are the only person capable of answering them."

Panther laughed.

"I find it difficult to believe that I am the sole source of the answers you seek," he said. "However, if you have questions for me, I'll do my best to answer them honestly."

"I expect nothing more."

"And nothing less, I suspect," Panther added. "What would you ask of me, sir?"

"We might begin, I suppose, with your name. Is it not Jones? It is common for young men born out of wedlock to take their mother's name, is it not?"

"I suppose so," said Panther, with a touch of exasperation in his voice. "Have you come merely to berate me for failure to conform to the standards of respectable society?"

"Not at all. It is unusual, but not illegal. I asked merely for my own edification."

"I have never been overly concerned with propriety," Panther said. "And Panther has been good for business. People remember it more easily than if my name were Jones."

"Would I be mistaken to assume that the name of Tecumseh, in the Shawnee language, translates to 'Panther' in English?"

"Actually, it's more like 'He Who Walks Like a Panther,'" Panther said. "But, no, you would not be mistaken in that assumption. What else?"

"These coughing fits. They seem to have come on you rather suddenly."

"Not as sudden as all that," Panther said. "But recently, nevertheless. I fear I'm not well. But never mind my affliction. What more do you wish to know?"

"Actually, the source of your affliction is another of the matters I wish to discuss," Beede said.

"And are you prepared to cure me of this? Are you a physician as well as a lawyer?" Panther asked.

"No, indeed," said Beede. "However, I've consulted with a physician, and I believe I've discerned your problem."

"And it is?"

"Arsenic poisoning," Beede said. "And I see from your face that you have come to a similar conclusion."

"Yes, I have," Panther said. "It is incurable, as you know. I've been exposed to far too much for far too long."

"Was it worth the sacrifice of your life?"

"Oh, yes," Panther said proudly. "Although I will most probably die from the exposure, I have lived to see the death of General Harrison. That alone makes the thing worthwhile."

He fell into another fit of coughing that continued for several minutes.

When the coughing subsided, Beede said, "Am I also correct in assuming that you killed General Harrison with arsenic?"

"You are," Panther said. "It took some little time to do, since I dared not move too quickly, but gardeners usually have arsenic around for dealing with rats. It was convenient that I was hired to do the planting on the grounds of the mansion, for it provided an excuse to be here every day. It was a simple matter to slip into the kitchen each morning as we worked and add a bit of poison to the general's food and drink."

"Thirty days seems hardly enough time to bring a man down with arsenic," Beede said.

"It isn't, as a rule. Fortunately, I had been employed by General Harrison at his property in Ohio for several months before his election, which probably helped me to obtain employment here. It was a nice irony, I thought, that General Harrison's good opinion of me helped put me in a position to carry out my plan to murder him."

"I don't understand why you did this," Beede said. "Surely the general had done nothing to you."

"To me, personally, no. But to my line, yes. I am Shawnee, as you may have perceived. Harrison destroyed the Shawnee."

"I thought originally that you were Negro."

"My mother was," Panther said. "Indians and Negroes often intermarry. In my mother's case, it was not marriage, but it had the same effect."

Beede thought. "You said Harrison destroyed the Shawnee, and yet they still live."

"They exist, but they do not live. They have been moved a thousand miles from their homeland. Broken in spirit, circumscribed by territorial limitations imposed upon them by others, subjugated by the white man and dependent on his largess—of which there is little enough. In their greed for land the white men destroyed a great nation, including the greatest man among us."

"Tecumseh?"

"Tecumseh, yes. I am his descendant. It was my destiny, from the day of my birth, to avenge his death."

"I fail to understand this passion of yours," Beede said. "You could hardly have known the great chief;

you would have been two or three years old, at most, when he died."

"I never knew him," Panther admitted. "But he is my ancestor. His blood runs in my veins."

"Not much of his blood. Your mother and your mother's father were both Negroes. Tecumseh died when you were very young. You could not be more than a distant relative."

"Do you think that matters?" Panther said. "White men may judge the purity of a man's heart by some arcane mathematical formula. Indians are not so naïve as all that. Tecumseh is my ancestor, and it was my calling to avenge his death. I have devoted all my energies to that end ever since I learned the truth regarding my ancestry."

"And when was that?"

"Two years ago," Panther said. "Just before my mother died, she told me how she had lain with the son of the great Tecumseh. I'd never heard of him before that moment, but she told me the tales of his great heart and his stirring achievements. How everyone who met him admired his fighting spirit, his leadership, his intelligence and wisdom."

This, Beede knew, was true, at least as far as the great chief was concerned. Even Harrison had said, and had been quoted to that effect on several occasions, that Tecumseh had been an extraordinarily effective leader who could probably have excelled in any situation in which he found himself. There were suggestions of these same traits in Panther, however distant the blood relationship might have been.

"But what will you do now?" Beede asked. "You

are a murderer, and will soon be known as a murderer. Even if you escape from me—and I doubt that you can—you will not escape forever. Justice may not be swift, but it is certain. It will inevitably catch up with you."

"I'm aware of that," Panther said. "Indeed, I believe it has caught up with me already. I am a dead man, or will soon be a dead man, as a consequence of working with arsenic these past few years. The white man can do nothing worse to me, try as he might."

"He will try, nevertheless," Beede said. "You will be arrested for the murder of the president, tried, and probably convicted. I will be obligated to testify at your trial and confirm the admissions you have made to me today."

"For that to occur," Panther replied, "it will be necessary to arrest me. I have six loyal men in my crew. You have no chance to best me without assistance, and I will not make it easier for you by surrendering."

"Then I shall go away and recruit reinforcements," Beede said. "It shall not take long."

T**he** task required more time than he had anticipated. It was complicated by the fact that Harrison's death had been widely attributed to pneumonia, and people were reluctant to make a false arrest.

Three hours later, having prevailed upon Webster to recruit a couple of men to assist him, Beede finally returned to the site where Panther's crew had been working. The little company found a full crew of workmen there, except for Panther. As Beede had feared, the young man was no longer present.

"He left a couple of hours ago," his second-in-command said. "He said he had some urgent business out west, again. Are you Josiah Beede?"

"Yes, I am."

"Charlie gave me a note to pass along to you."

The note said that Panther was bound for Kentucky once more to "finish up the Tecumseh business."

"No need to follow me," the note said. "I'll be back as soon as I'm finished in Kentucky."

"What's he mean by that?" asked a member of the posse. "What urgent business did he have in Kentucky?"

"He's planning to kill Colonel Johnson, I believe," Beede said. "Johnson's the man who really killed Tecumseh."

"Do you suppose he'll really come back? If he's committed another murder after this one, why would he return?"

"Strangely enough, I believe he will," Beede said. "But I must follow him. I've no intention of letting him get away with another homicide."

There was railroad service to New England now, but there was none to Kentucky, and little enough stagecoach service. River travel would be unpredictable at best, now that summer was approaching and the water level was dropping in the rivers. Beede did the best he could and booked passage on a coach leaving at noon the following day. In the meantime, he took a room in a hotel and attempted to sleep. It would be hard to sleep well in a stagecoach, jammed shoulder to shoulder with humanity, and he needed to gain as much rest as possible in the hours remaining before departure.

Before retiring, however, he acquired paper and pen and composed a letter to Deborah. It was more difficult than he had anticipated, perhaps the most difficult letter he had ever attempted to write. In the letter he told her of his love, apologized for his absence, and assured her that he would return to New Hampshire as quickly as possible. He explained his mission briefly and explained why it was important, and he left it at the front desk to go out in the next post.

Would it be adequate to the task? Would it restore him to her good graces? He could only hope. In the meantime, he had a job to do.

Spring was melding slowly into summer, so Beede's second trip to Kentucky was a bit faster than his first. It was less comfortable, traveling by stagecoach through the ruts and the dusty western roads. It was, however, more direct. He arrived in Frankfort in a little more than five days.

He went immediately to the tavern where he had met previously with Colonel Johnson. He was in luck; the former vice president was sitting at a table in the far corner of the taproom. Panther had not yet succeeded in killing him.

"I've not heard the name before," Johnson said when Beede inquired. "He wants to kill me, you say? Well, it's been tried before, without much success."

"He succeeded with General Harrison," Beede said.

Johnson thought for a moment.

"I suppose you're right," he said finally. "I think I'm in much better shape than the old general was, but I take your point. What would you have me do?"

"Lend me a man or two," Beede said. "If Panther is nearby, we will find him and bring him to justice."

Johnson lent two men to Beede, both of them slaves. Beede was uncomfortable making use of such men, but he saw no alternative.

In reality, both men were quite helpful. They were an odd pair: an older man with a gray curling beard who moved slowly and rheumatically, and a younger, shorter man with a lighter, almost olive complexion. Neither seemed enthusiastic about their mission, but neither did they object to it. Beede wondered about Johnson's private opinion of this endeavor; more than that, he wondered about the slaves' opinions. Were they emotionally engaged in the search for Charles Panther, the man who intended to kill their master, or were they secretly in sympathy with his intentions? Beede found it difficult to believe that they were impartial about the matter.

The search took several days and ranged farther and farther from Frankfort. They traveled on horseback, following the Kentucky River downstream almost to the Ohio, asking discreet questions along the way of shopkeepers and publicans.

It was the older slave, Henry, who tracked down

their quarry. Panther had been found lying beside the road nearly a fortnight before, Henry said, and had been taken in by a free colored family.

"He ain't gettin' any better," Henry said. "Fact is, if he was improvin', they wouldna tole me where he was, I don't think. They knowed I was workin' for a white man."

"Why did they change their minds?"

"Like I said, he ain't getting' any better. They don't think he'll last much longer. They just wants to see him git some help."

"Do they know I want to take him back to Washington and put him in jail?"

"They knows," Henry said. "But they don't believe he'll make it that far. He's too weak."

Beede, when he was finally allowed to see Panther, could only agree with that assessment. The young man had been propped up in bed, which seemed to be all that was keeping him upright.

"Well, Mr. Beede, you followed me after all," he said.

"As you knew I would."

"Knew?" Panther said. "I hoped, certainly, that you would be present to witness my triumph. Instead, I suppose you will witness my defeat. I fear I shall never leave this bed alive."

"I think you were counting on my arrival in time to prevent you from engaging in this folly," Beede said. "I cannot believe you desired the death of Colonel Johnson any more than you truly desired the death of President Harrison."

"Then you would be wrong, sir," Panther said.

"You are wrong at least as far as General Harrison was concerned. All through his presidential campaign I sought—and achieved—employment in the Harrison household. It offered me the opportunity to poison him slowly, over an extended period of time, which is generally believed to be the most effective method for killing a man with arsenic. Fortunately, arsenic is always around, and it seemed appropriate in this instance. I have not borne such enmity for any man as I bore for him. He prevailed through cowardice and treachery and grew in stature and reputation through the ills he inflicted on others; he was without honor."

"Cowardice? Treachery? How so?"

"He dissembled at every opportunity. He cheated the Indians of their lands. All Indians—not merely Shawnee. He knew Tecumseh would be a formidable negotiator, so he waited until the Great Chief was away to make his deals."

"And Colonel Johnson?"

"He killed the Great Chief in face-to-face combat. He deserves to die, but he should die like a hero. My intention was to kill him in combat. Not by poison." He sighed mightily. "I fear now that I must leave that task to someone else."

"I understand," Beede said. "I cannot share your sentiment, but I can understand your sense of failure."

"It's true that I have failed," Panther said, with unexpected fervor. "But I have done all I could humanly do. The great Tecumseh told his people to live in such a way that they need not fear death. 'Do not beg for more time to live your life over,' he said. 'Sing your death song and die like a hero.' I intend to do as he instructed."

"A difficult challenge," Beede said.

"Difficult, indeed," Panther replied. "It is the hardest thing I have ever done."

"**H**enry tells me your rogue Indian is dead," Johnson said when he met with Beede at the tavern several days later. "Why'd he want to kill me, anyway?"

"He believed himself to be a descendant of Tecumseh," Beede said. "He thought it was his duty to avenge his death."

"Revenge, huh?" Johnson mused on this. "I can't say I blame him much, I guess. Awful glad he didn't get the chance, though."

"He wanted to kill you in face-to-face combat," Beede said. "He killed Harrison—or believes he killed Harrison—with arsenic, but he thought you deserved to know your assassin. He believed the struggle would be fairer, I suppose, if it were face to face."

"Fair?" Johnson echoed. "I'm sixty-one, and he was, what, early thirties? I've been sitting on my butt in the legislature, and he'd been working outdoors every day, building up a good set of muscles. Don't seem all that fair, when you look at it."

"He'd been slowly poisoning himself with arsenic however," Beede reminded Johnson. "The poison had sapped much of his strength. When I saw him last he was a mere shadow of the man I had met earlier."

"The same could be said of me, though not from arsenic," Johnson said. "Well, war ain't often fair, and I guess this was a form of war. I ain't about to complain about what's fair and what's not."

Chapter 26

Having completed his business in Kentucky, Beede returned to Warrensboro as quickly as he could, hoping to arrive in time to render assistance to Randolph. He had no doubts that assistance would be needed—that Devall was somewhere nearby busily recruiting a vigilante band for another attempt at abduction. Devall returned to Warrensboro, with a larger contingent, on an afternoon in late June, but Beede and Randolph were prepared for him. It had been a couple of weeks since he had last appeared, and Beede and Randolph had spent the interval since Beede's return from Kentucky recruiting assistance. Ever watchful, Randolph confined his work to fields nearest his house. They had assumed that Devall would return with a larger force than in the past, perhaps recruited from as far away as Worcester and Boston.

A prearranged signal had been devised for this eventuality. A basket of pine needles was stored in Randolph's house. When Devall finally appeared one afternoon, Randolph threw handfuls of needles onto the smoldering fireplace coals. Thick black smoke erupted and poured up the chimney, alerting Beede and his neighbors. The first arrivals appeared in a few minutes, armed with rifles, shotguns, and, in some instances, pitchforks.

Beede walked in front of the crowd and spoke to Devall.

"We will not permit you to do this," he said.

"You cannot prevent it," Devall replied. "I have enough force to overpower you. Moreover, I have authorization from the governor."

"The governor has no power in this matter," Beede said. "Randolph is a free man, legally, and cannot be taken against his will, no matter what the governor says. And as for your rabble, we shall see how devoted they remain when the shooting begins."

"You won't shoot us," Devall said. "Not over a nigger."

As if in answer to his assertion, the sound of a flintlock hammer being cocked was heard from among the crowd of townspeople.

"In the past, you might have been accurate in your assessment," Beede said, calmly. "But Randolph has lived among us for several years and has been a good friend and neighbor. We would be loathe to lose him."

"Especially to a slaver," someone in the crowd said.

"Go home," said another. "We don't want you here!"

"I got a legal right to reclaim my property," Devall shouted. "These folks—Yankees, just like you—came here with me to make sure I get what's comin' to me. Now, you stand aside and let me claim what's mine, and I'll be out of your way!"

There were mumblings of dissent in the crowd, and Beede sensed that Devall had made some inroads. Randolph might be a neighbor, but he was also a colored man. Beede could sense the crowd's thoughts: was it wise to defy this armed mob in defense of a former slave?

Something needed to be done before Devall swept the field. Beede nervously scanned the faces of the crowd and saw, with sinking heart, that Devall's appeal was having its effect. The irony of the situation struck him; some in the crowd were as dark, or nearly as dark, as Randolph. Many were darker than Louisa. But because they were considered "white," they had no fears for themselves and, consequently, only limited sympathy for Randolph.

An idea occurred to him. He had only a split second to consider it, but he decided it was worth the chance.

"Why have you selected Randolph?" Beede asked Devall. "What makes you think he's a slave?"

"Look at him!" Devall replied. "All you have to do is look at him! He's a nigger, plain as day!"

"What about Jed Harris, here?" Beede asked,

pointing to one of the townspeople who had responded to Randolph's alarm. "Is he a Negro, too?"

"I'm Scotch," Harris said. "Always have been."

"But can you prove it?"

"Don't need to prove it! I been Scotch all my life, and my daddy before me. What're you saying?"

"But can you prove it? Randolph has a document that proves he's a free man. What do you have?"

He turned to another in the crowd. "How about you, Elijah? Can you prove you're a free man?"

"I'm Irish!" Elijah Whitmore said, hotly.

"You're what they call 'Black Irish,'" Beede said. "You're very dark, which has always made you popular with young women. But how do we know you're not really a Negro?"

"You've known me for years!" Whitmore shouted. "Was I ever a slave since you've known me?"

"I've known Randolph longer," Beede said. "I've known he was a free man for five years, and I know it to be true because I freed him myself."

To the rest of the crowd, he said, "You have known Randolph as long as you've known me. We arrived here together. You have accepted him as a free man. He has helped you with planting and harvest, with barn raising, and husking, like a free man. He has never given you any cause to suspect he is not free. Why would you now suspect otherwise, simply because a stranger comes upon us with an armed mob?"

The rumbling began, and it sounded, to Beede, like music.

"What do you know about this man?" he said, indicating Devall. "You know nothing. But I can tell you about him because I have met him before. He is a slave trader. He captures men and women—and children—and ships them to the South to work on the cotton and sugar plantations. There is no escape from these places.

"But this man does not share their fate. He comes and goes as he pleases, and he emerges wealthier than before. He is a man without principle or scruple, and he is not worthy of your consideration."

His remarks were having the desired effect, Beede saw. Some members of Devall's "posse" were muttering among themselves, and the townspeople were growing restless.

"You lie!" shouted Devall. "I will prove that you lie! Choose your weapon, and I will meet you in the field! If you refuse my challenge, you will stand unmasked as a liar and a coward!"

"We do not duel here," Beede said, calmly. "This is not the South. I would not accept your challenge, in any event. You are a man without honor and unworthy. No man who deals in the bodies and souls of his fellow man can be a man of honor. I would no more meet you on the dueling ground than I would a whoremonger."

Several men seized Devall before he could attack Beede, and Beede was pleased to see that the captors included two of Devall's own men. As they held the slaver fast in their grasp, Beede took advantage of the confusion.

"Go home!" he said to the crowd. "There is nothing for you, here."

For a few minutes the crowd milled around in con-

fusion while Devall sputtered in rage. Eventually,
everyone drifted away, and Devall's captors released
him. Beede prepared himself for an attack, but it did
not come. Instead, Devall approached him with
empty hands.

"I shall go now," he said. "But I will be back, and
you will regret your actions today."

"I shall continue to hope that you will come to a
change of heart, yourself," Beede replied.

The man was unmoved. "You may wish whatever
you prefer, until I return."

Beede thought long and hard about Devall's parting message. What, he wondered, could Devall
do that he had not already attempted? He could return
with a larger crowd of rabble, but he had no surety
that a larger mob would be more effective than this.
Further, the larger the throng the more attention it
would call to itself. New England was not as strongly
abolitionist as southern planters sometimes claimed,
but it would not do to provoke such sentiments
among a quiescent population.

He concluded, inevitably, that Devall was issuing
idle threats. There was little—perhaps nothing—the
man could do to follow through on his promise. He
supposed the governor could send militia to back up
Devall's demands, but he thought it unlikely for him
to weigh in on the side of the slavers, as it would be
politically risky. Governor Page was a Democrat and
a Jackson man, like most New Hampshire officehold-

ers, but he was not known as a particularly strong pro-slavery advocate.

Beede put the matter out of his mind and went on to a more pressing matter: marriage.

Chapter 27

"Yes, of course," said Deborah Tomkins Turner. "If you are certain that you desire to marry me, I will be happy to marry you."

"Then with your permission I will ask your father for your hand," Beede said.

"You may, if you wish," said Deborah. "But it is unnecessary. I can assure you that his consent is a foregone conclusion. As a matter of fact, he has been hinting, as subtly as he can, that I should make the first move. I believe he is growing impatient for grandchildren."

"I believe I should go through the formalities, in any event," Beede said. "It's always good to have the approval of all parties when one takes such an important step. Assuming his consent, when should we wed?"

"Soon," she said, firmly. "Who knows when duty will call you from me again. The demands on your time seem endless."

•   •   •

The wedding took place a week later, once again in the parlor of the Tomkins house. Few guests attended, which was as both Josiah and Deborah wanted it. Both had, after all, been married before. Deborah's younger sister, Sally, played the piano. The Reverend Nathaniel Gray performed the ceremony—reluctantly, Beede thought—and Randolph and Louisa were guests. The younger Tomkins children cared for Nancy in another part of the house.

Beede and Randolph had previously discussed the wisdom of asking Gray to officiate, given what they knew of his sentiments, but there was no one else to turn to for twenty or thirty miles. In addition, Deborah pointed out, to call in another minister would certainly rouse suspicions, not least in the mind of Mr. Gray himself.

So Gray read the ceremony, Beede and Deborah took their vows, and the newlyweds departed as soon as seemed proper. They went only as far as Deborah's house in West Warrensboro. Beede would have preferred to take her to his own house, but the hired crew of itinerant farm workers was living there. Beede supposed that he could have evicted them, now that he was back in town, but he could not bring himself to do so.

And in any event, the Turner house—Deborah's house—was more than adequate for two people to get to know each other better.

They went to bed even before the sun had set. It was summer, after all, and sunset was quite late.

Chapter 28

New England celebrated few holidays, and only three of them—Thanksgiving, Independence Day, and George Washington's birthday—were considered to be serious holidays, worthy of all-out revelry. The Fourth of July was announced to the citizens of Warrensboro, New Hampshire, while the sun was still creeping over the horizon, by the popping of firecrackers and the firing of muskets. Some of the older boys in the community had acquired the firecrackers, by some method they did not care to discuss, and had determined that they would awaken the townspeople to the dawning of the special day.

The cracker barrage was soon followed by the ringing of bells. Warrensboro had only two churches: the Center Congregational Church, which most people still called "the meeting house," and a small

Methodist chapel located by the creek that skirted the center village. The cacophony for which they were responsible, however, would have left visitors with the sense that the town was overrun with houses of worship.

Following the bells, the town began waking and preparing to meet the day. All but the absolutely essential chores—milking, for example, as it could not be avoided without dire consequences—were put aside for the day in favor of militia musters on the common and large-scale eating.

Mr. and Mrs. Josiah Beede remained in bed until the noise of cannon fire and of small boys banging out martial rhythms on tin pails made it unbearable to continue. It had been barely a week since their wedding.

Beede had never missed an occasion to turn out for musters, for he felt that his service in New Orleans— misguided as it was—had left him with a reputation that he must live up to. On this particular occasion, lying peacefully in his bed with his new bride at his side, he wished that he could remain where he was and let the festivities proceed without him.

He knew, however, that it was not to be. As if to underscore that fact, Deborah awakened at that moment and lay there smiling at him.

"Good morning."

"And good morning to you," he said, smiling. They were still behaving rather formally with each other, and he hoped that they might close that emotional distance eventually. He knew, however, of married couples who had maintained a formal relationship all their married lives and would probably continue to do so on their deathbeds.

"It is the Fourth," Deborah said.

"Yes."

"Do you feel you are obligated to muster with the others?" she asked. "Might you not remain with me?"

"I would love to," he said, "but I dare not. Your father will be expecting me to appear for the drill. It's a duty."

She giggled. He had never heard her giggle before, and he was surprised to find it charming.

"What is so amusing?" he asked.

"I was merely imagining the Warrensboro militia protecting the town from the enemy," she said merrily. "I believe we would be in greater danger from the militia."

"I regret to say that you are probably right," he said, laughing. "Perhaps if we drill long and hard today, we'll be able to minimize the risk of danger to ourselves and to our loved ones."

"And am I your loved one?"

He leaned over to kiss her. She responded with eagerness, and he decided that he need not leave the house for a little while yet.

At ten minutes to eleven—the muster was scheduled to begin at eleven—Warrensboro's citizen soldiers were treated to the sight of Josiah Beede dashing across the common to take his place in formation. Most of the guardsmen pretended to be unaware of his belated arrival, but Beede was certain they were fighting to prevent grins from spreading across their faces.

Militia musters were notoriously lax affairs, and Warrensboro's muster was no exception. Beede's own military experience, though limited to his brief foray in New Orleans, had been sufficient to cause him embarrassment at the ragged formations and the out-of-step marching. He had to admit to himself, however, that he was every bit as ragged as the least experienced member.

But the unit made up for its incompetence in military drill by its marksmanship. Beede had often marveled at the sharpshooting of the backwoodsmen who had come to New Orleans—the Creoles called them "Kaintucks"—bearing their squirrel rifles. The rifles, and their skill with them, had enabled them to pick off British infantry at a distance of three hundred yards, long before the redcoats could bring their smooth-bore muskets to bear.

In the intervening years, however, the advantages of rifled barrels had become apparent to nearly everyone who valued accuracy and frugality. Several members of the Warrensboro militia had acquired long rifles, much like those the Kaintucks had used, and the militiamen's marksmanship had improved considerably. Beede had recently been thinking that he should acquire a rifle for himself. He was proficient with a musket, but he also remembered his favorable impressions of the long rifles he had fired at New Orleans.

The sun rose higher in the sky, bringing with it an intense summer heat. Barrels of water had been set at various places along the drill field, but a number of militiamen had augmented the water with barrels of rum. The citizen soldiers turned increasingly to the rum barrels as the morning wore on. As a result, marchers began dropping out of the formations. Some simply surrendered to the sun and heat; those could be found lolling in the shade with friends while the others marched on. The more resolute marchers continued their drill until they stumbled in their tracks and crumpled to the ground, where merciful townspeople would rush onto the field and drag the casualties to safety.

Beede remained as long as he thought he was able, but he, too, was forced eventually to admit defeat. He had drunk little rum—not his favorite beverage—but the experiences of those around him would have discouraged him from imbibing too freely in any event. After an hour on the field, he staggered off to the sidelines and collapsed on one of the few patches of grass—and shade—that remained.

He looked around for Deborah, but she was not to be seen. A substantial crowd of spectators had gathered at the start of the drill, but it had dissipated quickly. Many of the spectators, he expected, had wandered across the Common to the meeting house, where Mr. Gray was scheduled to preside over the day's official ceremonies. Perhaps Deborah had gone there, as well.

As he crossed the common, however, he caught a furtive movement from the corner of his eye. A man, whom Beede recognized instantly, was moving toward the meeting house. When he arrived, rather than entering through the front, the man slipped around the side of the building toward where Beede knew the rear entrance lay.

So Devall had not left the town after all, as Beede had hoped. Or if he had, he had now returned.

Deborah, if she were in the meeting house, would have to wait a bit before he could join her. Beede followed in the direction Devall had gone. It took only a few minutes to discern that Devall was bound for Beede's house or, more likely, Randolph's.

Beede ran as fast as he could, taking some paths that only local people would know, in order to arrive before Devall. The family had arrived back home from the festivities only a few minutes earlier, and they were not eager to leave again immediately. Beede prevailed upon them, however, and Randolph saw the logic in escape.

"We'll go to the Turner farm," Beede said. "It belongs to Deborah, now. You should be safe there. I'll find Deborah and we will accompany you."

Beede found Deborah in the meeting house, and she hastened to join the group. They gathered a few belongings, hastily, and vacated the farm. None in the little party noted that they were observed by a short, pudgy man with a pencil moustache.

Chapter 29

Three-year-old Nancy awakened in total darkness, in an unfamiliar room, and wondered where she was. It came to her after a moment: she was in the house belonging to Father's friend, Mr. Beede, and his new wife, Deborah.

Her sense of panic subsided. She was safe. These were people she knew, and liked, and trusted. She was aware that many things went on about her that she did not understand, and recently she had sensed that all was not as it should be. Father and Mother were distant, as if something worried them. She had no idea what it might be, but it had instilled in her an indefinable sense of fear that had begun to eat away at her stomach.

But they had all come to visit Mr. Beede, so things must be all right. She even had her own bed—not a bed, precisely, but a pallet on the floor in the same room as Mother and Father. She could hear them both snoring nearby.

She lay quietly and listened, the peaceful sound filling her with tranquility, calming her anxiety. If they thought danger was near, her parents would not be sleeping so serenely.

She thought about the events of the exciting day she had just been through. There had been loud noises and explosions of various sorts, which had at first frightened her until Father had assured her that everything was all right. There were soldiers marching on the Green—funny-looking soldiers in all manner of dress. And a band playing loud music and often marching with the soldiers in that curious stumbling way. She had hardly been able to refrain from laughing, it was so funny.

And then there was the hustle and bustle of a quick departure, when Father and Mother packed bags of clothing and sneaked out of town, and Mr. Beede and Deborah joined them, and they walked and walked for what seemed like hours. Father and Mr. Beede kept looking over their shoulders as if expecting someone to join them.

Perhaps, she thought, they were looking for the little fat man who had been watching them in secret as they had prepared to leave. She had seen him once as they left town. He was peeking out from behind a rain barrel, and when she smiled at him he returned the smile before putting a finger to his lips in a shushing gesture.

He must be planning a surprise, she thought. She

wondered for whom. Mr. Beede and Deborah, perhaps? They were newly married, and people seemed to like to pay surprises on newlywed couples. The thought made her smile.

The best part of the day, however, had been riding Peter, Mr. Beede's horse. She had never ridden on a horse before, and she had thought that she might be scared. But it was wonderful. Father had hoisted her up, and Mr. Beede had held the reins, and Peter had walked placidly behind with Nancy on his back. She had anticipated that Father might join her on the horse, but he did not. He merely walked beside her, smiling and talking quietly to her.

In a short time, she forgot her fears and began to take in the view. She was so high in the air! She was above Father and Mr. Beede. She was above Mother and Deborah. She could look down on them, just like the birds. And she could see so far from there. She could see a farmhouse up ahead of them.

And when she looked behind them, over her shoulder, she saw, briefly, the little fat man again, partly concealed behind a tree. She smiled to herself and wondered what his surprise would be.

But there had been no surprise, apparently, because she did not see the man again. They arrived at the farmhouse and prepared for spending the night, eating some bread and cheese that they had brought along for supper. All through the meal she gazed anxiously at the door, expecting to hear a knock on the door at any time that would reveal the little fat man and his surprise.

After their supper, she and Mother went upstairs and to bed. Deborah came, too. Father remained downstairs, and she could hear him talking quietly with Mr. Beede. She strained to listen, but she could make out only a few, disjointed words before she was overcome by the excitement of the day. She fell asleep, dreaming of tomorrow.

But now she was awake again, and she wondered why that would be. She rarely woke at night; the excitement and adventures of the daytime usually caused her to sleep soundly until morning. She was vaguely conscious of a sound that she had heard before, which had brought her to full consciousness.

Something in the barn.

It was Peter, Mr. Beede's Morgan horse, she decided. Something was upsetting him. She could hear him prancing, moving restlessly in his stall. Someone should go to him, comfort him, calm him down. Horses also needed their sleep.

She became very still, listening for the sounds of an adult rising from bed and descending the stairs.

Nothing. The house was quiet.

Should she wake someone? No. It was time that she took some responsibility on her own, she decided. Peter was fond of her, and she was fond of Peter. She was still small, and there were many things she could not yet do, but this was within her range of skills. Peter would grow quiet when he saw her and heard her voice. She would make it a point to speak soothingly to him. Wouldn't Mother and Father be proud of her in the morning when they learned how she had taken this task on by herself?

Quietly, in order not to wake the household, she slipped down the stairs and raised the string latch on the front door. She padded across the farmyard to the barn, where the horse seemed even more agitated than before. The straw strewn on the dirt floor tickled her feet, but she stifled her giggle. It would not do to startle poor Peter. She could see him in his stall now, wide-eyed, ears pricked, dancing nervously and making soft whinnying noises. She opened the door to the stall, speaking quietly to the animal, which calmed him for a moment.

But only for a moment. He was soon prancing wildly again, snorting and trembling, and in a moment she realized the reason for his fear.

Smoke. The barn was on fire.

She knew enough of fire to realize the danger. She reached up to grab the halter rope but discovered it was tied to the stall door. She had never seen a horse tied up in the stall before, and she wondered, as she struggled to untie it, why it had been done. Surely not to prevent escape; the barn was secure, the planks sound, the stall firmly built.

She struggled with the knot in a growing frenzy, but to no avail. Her fingers were not strong enough; she succeeded only in causing them to bleed, which made it ever more difficult as her hand slipped on the knot.

She would need help. It was time to rush to the house and wake the others. Someone would be able to do what she could not.

She stroked the horse for a moment to calm his panic before turning to the barn door to make her escape. But as she began moving toward the door she heard a thump that she recognized—with horror—as the sound of the wooden bar slipping into place to hold the door shut from the outside.

So someone was there! She ran to the door, hammering it with her tiny fists and crying for help. The smoke was growing thicker. It filled her lungs and caused her to cough violently. She could not speak, now; she could only croak pitifully.

In a moment, she heard footsteps hurrying away, and then there were no sounds except the whinnying and thumping of the horse and the crackling of the flames.

Chapter 30

In Beede's dream, a horse was neighing. It was more than a neigh, almost a shriek of terror. Gradually Beede became aware that what he was hearing was not a dream, but reality. He awakened with a start and a single thought.

Peter! His little Morgan horse was, at this point, the only animal in the barn.

Not bothering to dress, he dashed down the stairs and out the door. It was clear that he was already too late. The building was engulfed in flame. He made an attempt to enter, but the heat and smoke were too intense.

At least, he thought, the house was in the village, close to neighbors, who came streaming out of their dwellings in varied states of dishabille. One of the townsmen immediately sized up the situation and organized a bucket brigade. It was clear that they had had considerable unfortunate experience with fire, for the brigade was in operation in only a few minutes. Beede joined in to haul water up from the well for the brigade to carry to the fire.

Randolph joined him in the bucket brigade and Beede nodded in grateful acknowledgement.

"I left Louisa asleep in bed," Randolph said. "If her help is needed, I'll wake her."

"Deborah, too, is asleep."

"How did this happen?" Randolph asked.

"I don't know. Everything was quiet when I went to bed."

"We won't be able to save the barn, I fear."

"No," Beede replied. "I am afraid not. We must put this fire down, however, or we'll lose the house as well."

Deborah appeared suddenly at his side.

"I smelled smoke and wondered what had occurred," she said. "How terrible!"

"Peter was in there," Beede told her. "He had no chance, I think."

"Have you seen Louisa?" Deborah asked. "I stopped by her room on my way, but she wasn't there."

"Randolph said she was still sleeping when he left her. Perhaps she's in with Nancy, comforting Nancy."

"I looked and Nancy is missing as well."

"Louisa must have come for her. We had better look for them, see that they're safe."

Despite his neighbors' desperate efforts, the attempt to save the barn was doomed to failure. The well soon ran dry, but even before then the fire was

long beyond help. The neighbors' efforts had prevented the fire from spreading to the house or, more
important, to neighboring farms, but the barn was
gone. With it went his horse.

When the sun rose the next morning, little of the
barn remained. Beede sat heavily on the doorstep
and fought back the tears as he mourned the animal.
The ruins still smoldered, and the remains were still
too hot to enter, but he could see the lifeless figure of
the horse lying where his stall had been. Not far away,
another lifeless shape—a smaller shape—lay forlornly
near the entrance. He could not make it out, but it
gave him a bad feeling.

"Have you seen Louisa?" Randolph asked. "I've
been back to the house, but our bed is empty."

"Deborah is searching for her now," Beede said.
"Nancy is missing, also."

"Do you suppose that this fire was started deliberately, perhaps by Devall, in order to divert our attention?" Randolph asked.

"The thought had occurred to me," Beede replied.
"While we were fighting the fire, he would have an
opportunity, perhaps, to abduct Louisa."

"And Nancy, too. It's certainly possible."

"I've searched everywhere I know," said Deborah,
returning. "Neither Louisa nor Nancy are anywhere to
be found."

"We think Devall abducted them," Randolph said,
his fists suddenly clenching.

"What can we do, then? We must not permit him to escape."

"We can only pray that it is not too late already," Beede said. "Fortunately, I suspect he has not left Warrensboro or has left only within the hour."

"Then where is he?" Randolph said. "Where should we look?"

"Let us begin," Beede said, "at the home of Pastor Gray."

"Josiah!" Deborah called. They turned to see her by the burned ruins of the barn.

"Have you found Louisa?" Randolph asked.

"No," said Deborah. "But I have found Nancy."

They found the girl in the ruined barn. Her body had been burned and blackened, and the smell of burnt flesh was redolent in the air. There was little doubt as to who the small figure had been.

"Oh, God," said Randolph, softly.

"Why was she in the barn?" Beede said.

"She came to comfort Peter, I suspect," Deborah said. "He would have been panicked by the fire. It's exactly what she would have done."

"It would have taken great courage," Beede said.

"Why did she not simply lead the horse to safety?" Randolph said. "I should have thought it was the logical course."

"She may not have thought the matter through," said Deborah. "She was surely frightened. It's difficult to think clearly when you are terrified."

"There's a bit of what appears to be a rope halter around Peter's neck," said Beede. "The other end of it is burned through. I think someone tied Peter to the stall. Nancy probably attempted to untie the knot but was unsuccessful. It must have been Devall's doing."

"Then he must have wanted the horse to die in the fire," Randolph said. "I'd not have credited it if I hadn't seen it. This is a truly evil man."

"I doubt that he expected Nancy to die, however," Beede said.

"Of course not," Randolph said bitterly. "She would have been a valuable property. He might not even have known she existed."

His voice broke suddenly, and Randolph turned away from the others. Deborah moved toward him to offer succor, but he turned back, wiping tears from his face.

"We had better go after Devall," he said. "I have no time for grief now. He killed Nancy and stole Louisa."

"You must grieve," said Deborah. "It is the natural thing to do."

"No," Randolph said. "First things first. I'll grieve tomorrow."

"Devall has Louisa," Deborah pointed out. "We cannot permit him to escape with her to the South. Go on. I'll see to readying Nancy for burial."

The journey back to the center village, where Nathaniel Gray's house and church were, was about five miles. It would have taken about twenty minutes at a gallop, but Beede no longer had a horse. As a consequence, it was more than an hour before Beede and Randolph arrived at Gray's parsonage.

Gray was not home. His wife met them at the door.

"He went out earlier in the evening and has not returned," Louisa Gray said. "Why do you seek him?"

"We have matters to discuss with him," Beede said. "Did he say where he was going?"

"No. Is he not at the meeting house?"

"I'll go look there," Randolph said. "Perhaps you had better stay here in the event he returns."

"Go quickly, then. Look for indications of where he might have gone."

"Do you always take orders from a colored man?" asked Mrs. Gray after Randolph had departed. "I would find that humiliating."

"When a man is as clever as Randolph, I would be a fool to ignore him," Beede said. "In truth, neither of us takes orders from the other. We are free men, both of us, but we often agree on a course of action because that course makes the greatest sense."

Louisa Gray rewarded this observation with a snort. "The fact remains," she said, "that man is a Negro." And she shut the door.

Would Randolph have more success at the meeting house? Before joining him, Beede thought, he should take steps to assure himself that the pastor was not simply hiding out in his own parsonage.

Circling the house on his way to the barn, he wondered if he were pursuing the wrong person. He had no doubts about Devall's intentions, but his suspicions of Gray were based entirely on circumstance. It was possible that he was mistaken about Gray's culpability in the efforts to capture Louisa and Randolph.

The problem was that Gray was the person most likely to be involved, and Beede could think of no other who fit the criterion as well as the pastor. Many New Englanders, it was true, harbored lukewarm feelings about slavery; many, in fact, nurtured pro-slavery sentiments. But few, he suspected, would be apt to act on those sentiments. To take action required a man of "principle," such as a minister of the gospel. Aside from himself and Randolph, Gray was the only person Beede knew who was aware of Devall's presence in Warrensboro.

The barn, much as he suspected, was not harboring a minister of the gospel. It housed a few horses, one of which he recognized as belonging to Mercy Gray, the pastor's daughter, who had in the past seemed to be interested in Beede as a potential suitor. No doubt that infatuation would pass away in time, and probably had already done so now that he was newly married to another. He was a bit surprised, however, that she had not come to the door with her mother in response to his knock, if only out of curiosity.

He glanced upward, unthinking, toward the rooms on the house's second floor, but caught himself doing so and quickly looked away again. It would not be appropriate to look at the room where a young woman might be sleeping. He reminded himself that he was a married man once more, and turned his gaze elsewhere.

In that moment, however, he thought he caught a glimpse of Mercy's face and blonde hair at an upstairs window.

Chapter 31

Beede spent a few additional minutes convincing himself that Pastor Gray was not about the premises before setting off in the direction of the meeting house. He met Randolph on the way.

"He is not there," Randolph said. "But he has been there, and recently. Mr. Skinner said he saw the pastor leaving as Skinner was closing his store. The pastor seemed a bit hurried, Skinner thought."

"Was Devall with him?"

"Skinner did not see him, nor did he see Louisa. Devall and the pastor might have been planning to meet somewhere outside the village."

"Where was the pastor bound?"

"Skinner said Pastor Gray seemed to be going south, which is, of course, not the direction of his house," Randolph said. "There's no doubt in my mind that Devall will be going south if he has abducted Louisa."

"He could board the railroad in Concord," Beede said. "And he could be in the South in a day."

"But the railroad would never permit Louisa to come aboard," Randolph pointed out. "Not unless she was passed off as someone's servant, and I don't believe Louisa would stand for that."

"She may not have a choice in the matter," Beede said. "All Devall has to do is declare that she is a fugitive from a plantation. From that point on, no one would listen to her protestations."

"We need horses if we are to apprehend Devall," Randolph said. "And we need to acquire them quickly."

They would also need assistance. Stephen Huff, the constable, would be duty-bound to assist them in the pursuit. If, in fact, Devall had managed to go beyond the outskirts of Warrensboro, Huff's intercession would be essential in dealing with other officers of the law in other jurisdictions.

Huff was not been eager to join the party, but Beede explained the situation—rather more forcefully than he had intended—and Huff recognized his responsibility. He arranged for the loan of two saddle horses for Beede and Randolph and quickly saddled his own mount.

"I find it difficult to imagine Pastor Gray's involvement in this matter," he said to Beede when they were on the road. "I grant you he's not captivated by members of the African race, but I can't see him taking a step such as this."

"I find it difficult to believe, also," Beede said. "But he is apparently in thrall to Louisa—not his wife, but Randolph's. Lust has led men to do irrational things in the past."

"And him a preacher, too," Huff said. "Well, Louisa's a pretty little thing, but I wonder if the pastor has taken leave of his senses."

They stopped at every tavern along the way. They were nearing Concord when Huff recognized the minister's horse hitched to a porch railing. There were two additional horses hitched nearby.

"I will go in the front door," Huff said. "Mr. Beede, why don't you wait outside in front in case they slip past me?"

"What about me?" Randolph asked.

"Go to the rear of the building and watch the back door," Huff said.

"Their horses are here in front," Beede said.

"But there is a stable full of horses in the rear," Huff pointed out. "Some might even be saddled, still."

"Try not to cause them to panic," Beede said. "We don't want them to take flight." Huff nodded and entered the tavern.

He returned after only a few minutes.

"Louisa is there," Huff said. "She is sitting with a short, heavy man, and I could see that she isn't happy about it."

"And Gray?"

"I see no sign of him. I'm going back inside, and I will endeavor to learn what I can from the two who remain."

"Be . . ."

"Do not concern yourself; I shall be careful," Huff said. "I'm aware of the risk involved."

Huff returned to the tavern, and Beede returned to pacing back and forth outside. He thought about where Gray might have gone.

Beede heard metal clicking on metal. He turned quickly to see Mercy Gray, the pastor's beautiful daughter, pointing an old flintlock musket at him.

"I'm afraid I must ask you to remain with me a while," she said. "I realize that this is a terrible burden on you, but I fear that I must insist."

Was the gun loaded and primed? He assumed that it was.

"Hardly a burden," he said. "To gaze upon a beautiful young lady, such as you."

A sigh of exasperation. "Please, Mr. Beede, do not patronize me. I offered you my heart, and you rejected it. To add insult to injury, you have married my rival. I can only assume that you find my presence intolerable."

"Hardly that," Beede said. "Deborah and I have had experiences that brought us closer together. In other circumstances, perhaps . . ."

"Of course," Mercy said, dryly. "Well, it no longer matters. Now I find you persecuting my father, and that is something I must prevent if I can. I am merely a woman, but I have learned to use a gun. I do not wish to shoot you, but I will not permit my father to be harmed."

"If he is harmed," Beede said, "it would not come

from me. But neither will I permit him to harm another, as he is apparently determined to do."

"My father," Mercy said, "could not harm anyone. He is kind and gentle. He is the most perfect man I have ever known. I thought once that you might be his rival in virtue, but I was mistaken."

She prodded Beede, gently but firmly, with the barrel of the musket.

"Come, sir. We will join your Negro friend in the stable."

With the musket barrel at his back, Beede led the way around the corner of the building. He found Randolph propped against a stable wall, hands tied behind his back, his feet tied together.

"I'm sorry, Josiah," Randolph said. "I let down my guard when I saw Miss Gray."

"As did I," Beede admitted. To Mercy, he said, "I must say I'm impressed that you overpowered Randolph and tied him up by yourself."

"Oh, I had help," Mercy said. "M'sieur Devall was with me, briefly. He is really quite resourceful."

"You know what he is," Beede said. "He's a slave catcher. He means to take Louisa—and probably Randolph—back to the South, where they will be sold into slavery once more."

"Of course," she said. "Do you think this disturbs me? It is what God intended. Negroes cannot endure as free people. They lack the intellectual capacity and the ambition to be successful without white men to spur them on. We are doing them a good turn."

"Randolph has done quite well on his own."

"But he had you," she replied. "I've no doubt you

have explained to him everything he needs to do in order to make his farm productive, and I don't doubt that you've forced him to work in order to accomplish everything he has done. It's common knowledge that Negroes are lazy and intellectually inferior to whites."

"I have been away from my farm more often than not," Beede said. "And while I have been away, Randolph has turned his property into a model for the entire community. My farm is being worked by five hired men who cannot accomplish everything that Randolph has done."

"I don't believe you."

"You need only compare my farm to his," Beede said. "I envy his diligence and yield to no man in my admiration of his good judgment."

"Pretty words," she said. "Pretty, but meaningless. Even if true, they say nothing about the woman, his concubine. Clearly, she is merely a temptress. A slutty woman placed here to lead moral men astray. I notice that he has not married this woman. Obviously, he believes she is not a suitable wife."

"She is quite suitable," said Randolph. "That is why I risked returning to the South to rescue her from slavery. I considered her my wife then; I consider her so today."

"I was there, also," Beede said. "We had dealings with this man, Devall, in New Orleans. He attempted to defraud the court there in order to place both Randolph and Louisa in slavery. The judge saw through his deception, and I believe a New Hampshire court would do the same."

"We could not be wed in Warrensboro because we could not find a minister willing to perform the ceremony," Randolph said. "We have been in correspondence with an African Methodist Episcopal church in Massachusetts, however, and we hope to be married there in the fall, after the harvest."

"Nevertheless, she must go," Mercy said. "Her presence here is disruptive of the proper order of things. She has worked her wiles on too many innocent men. If she were to remain in Warrensboro, no good would come of it. My father is an upright moral man, but she tempts him almost beyond endurance."

"And how does she do that?" Beede said, mildly.

"Her mere presence reeks of carnality and lust. No man can resist the devil forever. It is unfortunate, but not surprising that my father has succumbed."

"*I* have not succumbed," Beede said. "I have been daily in her presence far longer than your father, and she has not dragged me into degradation. I enjoy her company, but I harbor no lustful desires toward her. How is it that I have resisted when your father has not?"

"Perhaps you have no manly desires," she said. "You resisted my charms, and I am considered uncommonly attractive, I believe."

"I suppose that must explain it," Beede said, but the sarcasm was lost on the minister's daughter.

"I must express my sympathies to poor Deborah," Mercy Gray said. "She has had terrible experience with husbands: first a corpse and then, apparently, a eunuch."

"Whether I am a eunuch will be apparent in time,"

Beede said. "I don't believe Deborah is concerned about it."

The tavern's back door opened suddenly, and Devall appeared. He grinned delightedly when he saw the situation that presented itself.

"Mr. Beede!" he said. "How magnificent it is to see you again! I had wondered whether we would have an opportunity to converse before I returned to the South. I should have had more faith in your resourcefulness."

"And Toby, too!" he said. "This is a pleasant surprise! You'll be pleased to know that you'll soon be reunited with your lovely Louisa! Not permanently, of course, but for the duration of our journey south."

"His name is Randolph," Beede said. "He is a free man, as is Louisa. If you take them from this place I will come after you."

"Oh, I dare say you will," Devall said. "It will be a fruitless journey, however, for you will never know where I have sent your friends. The South is a big place, and you shall have considerable difficulty finding me, not to mention those to whom I have sold them."

"It's no use, Josiah," said Randolph. "He'll send us south to the sugar plantations. By the time you find us, we could be dead."

"That's certainly a possibility," Devall admitted. "It would be unfortunate if that were the case—especially if it meant the loss of such a lovely woman as Louisa—but we must all make the best of the cards life deals us. I suspect the sugar plantations would be the best place for you, but I believe I can find a higher use for Louisa. I might even keep her for myself. After all the trouble she's put me through, I feel the need for compensation."

It occurred to Beede that Louisa was not present. She had been with Devall in the tavern, but Devall had emerged alone. For that matter, where was Constable Huff?

Devall apparently read his mind.

"No doubt you're wondering where your friend the constable is," he said. "He's really very clumsy at deception, I'm afraid. I saw through his masquerade almost immediately. It was a simple matter to distract him long enough for Mr. Gray to subdue him. I took your constable outside and tied him to a tree some distance from here. When he awakens he'll wonder where he is. I left Mr. Gray to guard Louisa until I return."

"No!" said Mercy Gray. "You cannot leave him alone with that . . . Jezebel! He's helpless in her spell!"

"That's certainly true," said Beede, spotting a ray of hope. "She is only too willing to lead him astray, and he's altogether willing to be led. They have probably escaped on their own, already." From the corner of his eye he could see that Randolph recognized his stratagem and did not intend to protest. Mercy Gray emitted a low moan.

"There's no reason to be concerned," Devall said, blithely. "Even if he uses her a little bit, what's the harm? In the end, I'm taking her with me."

"You," said Mercy Gray, "are a stupid, stupid

man!" Taking the gun with her she broke into a run for the tavern door.

Beede moved quickly before Devall could react effectively. As the little man moved toward the tavern in pursuit of Mercy, Beede tackled him from behind and brought him sprawling to the ground. To his surprise, he found Randolph beside him sitting on the little fat man.

"I've been working on my bonds for a while," he said. "I had my hands free some time ago, but I couldn't get to my legs until this little contretemps distracted their attention."

"Well, let's tie him and deliver him to Constable Huff," Beede said. "Then we'll need to determine where they have taken Louisa."

"No," said Randolph. "After we find the constable, let's take Devall with us. I'd feel better if I knew where he is at every moment."

Chapter 32

Huff was, as Devall had said, tied to a tree, groggy and in considerable pain, but awake. Huff would have killed Devall on the spot but for Beede and Randolph, who convinced him that more important duties lay ahead. They acquired horses from the tavern keeper and rode off in pursuit.

"Where could they be bound?" Huff said.

"South," said Randolph. "Anywhere in the slave territories will do, I suspect."

"Mr. Gray has no slaveholding interests," said Huff. "What good will it do him to go there?"

"I told him I could acquire land for him," Devall said, bitterly. "I told him he could make Louisa his servant—his very special servant—once he was established in the South. The idea seemed to appeal to him."

"And he would abandon his wife, his family, his calling for that?"

"You've seen Louisa," Devall replied. "What do you think?"

"But . . . a minister of the gospel!"

"Many ministers in the South own slaves," Devall said. "They don't seem to be riven with guilt about it. Things are simpler in the South, and I can't wait to return."

"You're going to spend a little more time here in the North," Huff said. "Several years, I'd wager."

Devall shrugged as if it made no difference to him.

"Tell me, for I must know," Beede said. "Why did you murder Frank Turner?"

"So you figured that out, did you?" Devall said. "I didn't intend to, but he began having second thoughts about our enterprise, even after I had promised him a one-third share of the profits from the sale of the slaves. Apparently he had married an ardent abolitionist, and she convinced him of the error of his ways. He said she seemed to have particular fondness for these two slaves."

The train had already left the station. The schedule posted on the depot wall indicated that they had missed it by ten minutes. Beede considered how they might overtake it but concluded it was—if not impossible—highly unlikely. Railway trains were known to reach speeds of fifteen to twenty miles per hour. No horse could maintain such speeds for more than a few minutes.

He said as much to Randolph.

"That has also occurred to me," Randolph replied.

"However, let us not jump to unwarranted conclusions. First let us be certain that they actually boarded the train."

"Do you believe they might not have boarded?"

"I believe Louisa would do all in her power to avoid it," he said. "She would consider a return to the South to be a sentence of death."

"But could she avoid it?"

"I hope so. Let us find out."

The shot rang out from a thicket about fifty yards away. Beede and Randolph began running in that direction while Huff remained behind to guard Devall. They arrived to find Nathaniel Gray lying on a bed of pine needles, bleeding profusely from the chest. Mercy sat nearby, dry-eyed but shaking, clutching the now useless musket.

"I wanted to kill the nigger whore," she said tonelessly, "but he would not permit it. He thought he was going to take her back to the South and possess her and have carnal knowledge of her. He attempted to wrest the gun from my hands."

"Where is Louisa?" Randolph said.

Mercy looked around curiously. She seemed stunned.

"I'll find her," Randolph said, ignoring her silence. He slipped away, and Beede was reminded of another time and place, when Randolph slipped almost noiselessly into the Louisiana swamp. He was searching for Louisa on that occasion, also.

A wagon was arranged to take the minister's body back to Warrensboro for burial. As the wagon driver

set off on the journey accompanied by Mercy, Randolph appeared with Louisa.

"She had not gone far," he said. "In truth, the most
difficult part of my task was not finding her but per-
suading her that she was safe. The New Orleans slave
market is still fresh in her memory."

When he saw that Louisa was a free woman again,
Devall argued that he, too, should be freed.

"You have no right to hold me here," he said to
Huff. "I did nothing illegal. It is not against the law to
try to recover my slave. Moreover, since I did not succeed, no harm has been done."

"That is not true," Beede said. "You burned down
Frank Turner's barn, killing my horse and Louisa's
three-year-old daughter."

"I would be happy to compensate you for the
horse," Devall said. "I did it only to distract attention
in order to capture Louisa."

"And the girl?"

"I did not know about the daughter," Devall said.
"I would not have killed her deliberately."

"Not even if the killing would demoralize Louisa
and make her more tractable?" Beede asked.

"Not even then," Devall replied. "Louisa would be
valuable, certainly, but a three-year-old girl who
looked like Louisa would be even more valuable in a
few years. I would not knowingly destroy such a po-
tentially valuable asset."

"I suppose not," said Beede, with disgust.

"What sort of man do you think I am?" Devall said
indignantly.

A blind rage overcame Beede. He reached Devall

in two strides and struck him hard enough to drive the little man back into the arms of Huff, who was in the process of tying Devall's hands behind his back.

"You are no sort of man," Beede said. "You are less than human. I think of you as something that lives under a rock. And when you are put away, as you should be, I shall not think of you ever again."

He prepared to strike again, but Randolph caught his arm and prevented it.

"Please don't," he said, quietly. "I feel as you do—even more so—but it isn't worth this. I have few enough friends in this world; I cannot afford to lose you. If you were to be convicted of an assault—even on scum such as this—my life, and Louisa's, would be in greater peril."

"Who's going to know?" said Huff. "They won't hear it from me. In fact, I might hit the son of a bitch myself."

"No," said Randolph. "If he is badly harmed, it could go hard on us. I've learned the hard way that there is no great reservoir of anti-slavery sentiment here. I cannot risk any action that might erode our popular support."

He turned to Beede again. "I told you once that I was not ready to call you by your Christian name. I believe you have shown yourself to be a true friend. Thank you, Josiah."

Devall was delivered to the jail in Concord. Beede did not know what fate would ultimately befall the slave trader, but he took consolation from the fact that Devall's scheme had been thwarted.

"You had better keep an eye open from now on," Beede told Randolph. "If Devall is freed, I doubt that he'll return, but he might send another slave catcher to finish the task."

"If he does so, his surrogate will receive a warm welcome," Randolph said. "I don't think the fact of Nancy's death has quite sunk in with Louisa, but once it has, I almost pity any man who comes to us with slavery on his mind."

Chapter 33

There would have to be one more journey to Washington City. Webster deserved to receive a final report on his investigation. Beede had been too concerned about Randolph to stop on his way back from Kentucky.

On this trip there was no cold supper in a darkened house by the President's Park. There was, in fact, no meal at all. The civility that Webster had displayed at their previous meetings was clearly strained on this occasion.

Webster himself greeted Beede at the front door— Beede assumed he had seen his approach—and ushered him quickly into a sitting room, where he closed and locked the door behind them.

"So you have come at last to disclose your findings, have you?" Webster said with a trace of exasperation in his voice. "What have you learned after all these three months?"

"I believe President Harrison was murdered, as you feared," Beede said. "The culprit died before I could bring him to justice."

"Since Mr. Tyler remains in office, I assume you did not assign the guilt to him."

"No," Beede said.

"Not in any sense?"

"Not at all."

"You suspected Senator Clay at one point," Webster said. "Do you still believe that he was involved?"

"I do not. General Harrison was poisoned by a descendant of the Shawnee chief, Tecumseh. The murderer found employment working on the grounds of the President's House and found a way to slip arsenic into his food and drink. He had previously worked for the general at his home in Ohio, so he had ample opportunity to do the deed over an extended period of time."

"Interesting," said Webster. "And you say the miscreant has died? Did he die by your hand?"

"By his own hand, actually. Years of working with arsenic finally took its toll. When I caught up with him in Kentucky, he was already on his deathbed."

"In Kentucky? Why was he in Kentucky?"

"Colonel Johnson had been the next man on his list," Beede said. "And Colonel Johnson returned to Kentucky after his term as Vice President ended."

"I see," Webster said, after a moment. "And you're certain of your conclusions?"

"All but one," Beede said. "General Harrison was

indeed a weakened, sickly man when he arrived in Washington, but it may not have been entirely the work of his enemy. It is possible that he would have died even without the poison."

"In other words, the president cooperated in his own death," Webster said, with a sigh. "Well, you'd better go see Senator Clay and tell him your story. He's been asking about you for a month."

"What do you intend to do with this information?"

"That, I think, will be Senator Clay's problem, not mine. Go tell him your story."

Clay was at home. He invited Beede into his house and listened without comment as Beede explained his findings.

"So, what you're telling me is that the general was not murdered by Tyler," Clay said. "Are you certain of this?"

"I had a confession from the man who did it," Beede said. "I believe it to be truthful."

"But I cannot question this alleged killer for myself, you say."

"Not by any means of which I'm aware. He is dead, now."

"Conveniently enough," Clay said. "Still, there's always the possibility that Tyler put him up to it, I'd think. After all, who would bear such animus against a man as harmless as the general. Don't you think Tyler . . ."

"No, I do not," Beede said firmly. "The murderer acted out of a desire for revenge on the man responsible for killing his precursor. I doubt that he would have agreed to be the instrument for another man's ambitions—especially not a white man's."

"And you say this all results from the death of Tecumseh."

"Yes."

"The Indian."

"Shawnee, yes."

Clay thought for a moment.

"And you've told all this to Webster?" he said, finally.

"I have."

"And he accepted your explanation?"

"Eventually."

"No doubt he was no happier than I," Clay said. "Well, Mr. Beede, please accept my thanks for your efforts on our behalf."

"Do you intend to announce that the general was murdered, then?"

"No," said Clay. "I do not. I've no wish to make the man a martyr, nor do I wish to provide aid and comfort to our enemies. Especially not to the Shawnee, who finally seem to be pacified. General Harrison is thought to have died of old age and pleurisy. That's good enough for me."

He turned without preamble and strode quickly to the door, which he opened. He looked back at Beede, who was standing, dumbfounded, in the middle of the room.

"Good day, Mr. Beede," said Henry Clay.

Afterword

American political parties have always taken a rather laissez-faire approach to ideology, but none, perhaps, was more casual than the Whigs. Although they borrowed the name of the British party that had supported the American cause during the Revolution, Whigs in America had little in common with their British counterparts or, for that matter, even with each other. The Whig Party in America included former Federalists, southern slaveholders, northern (and southern) abolitionists, northern industrialists, and occasional mavericks like Davy Crockett, whose political philosophy could not easily be explained. Whigs were nationalists, who favored a strong and active federal government, and regionalists, who believed that the federal government should be severely constrained by the states.

The one overriding point of consensus seems to have been personal and political animosity toward Andrew Jackson. John Tyler was, in nearly every respect, a states' rights, pro-slavery Democrat, but his distaste for Jackson seemed to cloud all other concerns in his mind. By allying himself with the Whigs, who boasted such ardent nationalists as Henry Clay and Daniel Webster, he virtually assured himself of no more than a single term in the President's House. If the party leadership had had its way, he would have been denied even that.

Of all the issues that divided the party, none was more divisive than slavery. It divided John Calhoun, a rabidly pro-slavery South Carolinian, from Henry Clay, a slave-holding abolitionist from Kentucky, from Daniel Webster, nominally an anti-slavery New Englander, whose personal convictions with regard to the South's "peculiar institution" seem to have been second in priority to his interest in national power. Small wonder that the party disintegrated during the decade preceding the Civil War, to be replaced by a new party—the Republican Party—with a clearer concept of its fundamental principles. The Whig Party was a party of anomalies.

Slavery also divided Democrats from each other, of course, but their party was spared, to some degree, the disaffection that spread like a pandemic through the Whigs. The Democratic Party's historical affiliations with Jefferson and Jackson, perhaps, provided it with archetypes that the newer party did not possess. Eventually the pro-slavery faction seemed to win out among Democrats, but there were always men like

Stephen Douglas among the party's ranks who were not personally opposed to slavery but who supported the Union nonetheless.

How do we make sense of this disparate conglomeration of political wills and egos? It is difficult to reconcile the conflicts that lay everywhere in the nineteenth century.

Richard Mentor Johnson is a prime example. A man of property—the primary source of nineteenth century wealth—he nevertheless flirted with bankruptcy through most of his life. A slaveholder in a slaveholding society, he nevertheless freed a female slave and made her his wife, raised their daughters, and promoted their advancement in white society. He also left them property of their own, which helped them to make advantageous marriages to white men.

In 1808, Congress took the first step toward outlawing slavery in the United States by prohibiting the international slave trade and penalizing American citizens who engaged in it. This was the first step, but it was merely the beginning of a long process. Far from shutting down the burgeoning commodity business in human beings, it had the immediate effect of increasing the market value of those slaves already in the system, and it increased the incentives for clever traders to create new slaves where they had not previously existed.

The South needed labor, and it preferred slave labor. When it was insufficient, or unavailable, it would make do with hired help, but slaves were the first choice. To meet this demand, a flourishing slave-catching industry arose in the United States. As a consequence, fugitive slaves could no longer be assured of safety anywhere in the United States.

Neither, for that matter, could free men of color. The northern, so-called "free" states, once a place of refuge, became a hunting ground for traffickers in human bodies. The difference between a free man of color and a slave, often, was completely in the hands of unscrupulous whites.

The enactment of a new fugitive slave law in 1850—a law far more oppressive than its 1793 predecessor—made conditions much worse and contributed in large measure to the regional divisions that brought on the Civil War a decade later. But that is another story.

THE JOSIAH BEEDE MYSTERY SERIES
by
Clyde Linsley

Death of a Mill Girl
0-425-18713-6

Saving Louisa
0-425-19309-8

"LINSLEY WRITES WITH A SPARSE ELEGANCE
REMINISCENT OF DICK FRANCIS."
—UNDER THE COVERS

"LINSLEY WEAVES THE FINEST THREADS OF
THE HISTORICAL MYSTERY...INTO AN
IRRESISTIBLE TAPESTRY."
—ANN McMILLAN

Meet Captain Gabriel Lacey in

The
Hanover Square
Affair

by
Ashley Gardner

IN WAR OR AT PEACE,
CAPTAIN LACEY KNOWS HIS DUTY.

His military career may have ended with an
injustice, but former cavalry officer Gabriel Lacey
refuses to allow others to share his fate.
The disappearance of a beautiful young woman
sets Lacey on the trail of an enigmatic
crime lord—and into a murder investigation.

0-425-19330-6

Also in the Regency England Mystery series:
A Regimental Murder
0-425-19612-7

Available wherever books are sold or at
www.penguin.com